D0696330

"Let's just forge[t] about last nigh[t]"

Kit wished desperately that he would go and leave her to her misery. The word "shame" was old-fashioned, she thought bitterly.

"And how am I supposed to do that?" Reid flushed angrily. "I've never been in this situation before. My experience—"

"Please." Kit wrenched her hand away. "Just drop it. You weren't to know."

"Ignorance is no excuse," he said quietly. He got up from the bedside. "Nonetheless I'll leave you alone, Katharine, since this is what you want. I'll be around all day if you need anything."

"Quite unnecessary, Reid. I'm in perfectly good hands—now."

The quiet, cruel little word hung in the air for several seconds before Reid abruptly went out and closed the door with a decisive click.

Books by Catherine George

HARLEQUIN PRESENTS
640—GILDED CAGE
698—IMPERFECT CHAPERONE

HARLEQUIN ROMANCES
2535—RELUCTANT PARAGON
2571—DREAM OF MIDSUMMER

These books may be available at your local bookseller.

For a free catalog listing all titles currently available,
send your name and address to:

Harlequin Reader Service
P.O. Box 52040, Phoenix, AZ 85072-2040
Canadian address: Stratford, Ontario N5A 6W2

CATHERINE GEORGE

imperfect chaperone

Harlequin Books

TORONTO • NEW YORK • LONDON
AMSTERDAM • PARIS • SYDNEY • HAMBURG
STOCKHOLM • ATHENS • TOKYO • MILAN

Harlequin Presents first edition June 1984
ISBN 0-373-10698-X

Original hardcover edition published in 1984
by Mills & Boon Limited

Copyright © 1984 by Catherine George. All rights reserved.
Philippine copyright 1984. Australian copyright 1984.
Except for use in any review, the reproduction or utilization of
this work in whole or in part in any form by any electronic,
mechanical or other means, now known or hereafter invented,
including xerography, photocopying and recording, or in any
information storage or retrieval system, is forbidden without
the permission of the publisher, Harlequin Enterprises Limited,
225 Duncan Mill Road, Don Mills, Ontario, Canada M3B 3K9.

All the characters in this book have no existence outside the
imagination of the author and have no relation whatsoever to
anyone bearing the same name or names. They are not even
distantly inspired by any individual known or unknown to the
author, and all the incidents are pure invention.

The Harlequin trademarks, consisting of the words
HARLEQUIN PRESENTS and the portrayal of a Harlequin,
are trademarks of Harlequin Enterprises Limited and are
registered in the Canada Trade Marks Office; the portrayal
of a Harlequin is registered in the United States Patent
and Trademark Office.

Printed in U.S.A.

CHAPTER ONE

'*PLEASE* say yes, Kit—*please*!'

Katharine Vaughan looked from one glowing, hopeful face to the other and shook her head.

'Sorry.'

'But Kit, think of it! Non-stop sunshine, cool, starry nights, and besides, you really need a holiday, you know you do. Please say you'll come!'

'Nothing doing. No way.' Kit remained unmoved.

Her twin sisters flopped disconsolately on the grass, their faces identical masks of despair. Kit's mouth twitched, but she suppressed a smile, refusing to meet two pairs of imploring cornflower blue eyes. Closing her own against the surprising warmth of a late September sun, she settled herself more comfortably on the garden lounger, trying to block her ears against the passionate duet of outpourings from her siblings, a pair never noted for restraint when trying to get their own way.

The bad fairy in their tale of woe was their friend Sandy, whose contraction of measles at the ripe old age of twenty was not only unforgivable but inconvenient. It ruled out the luckless Sandy from a holiday in Spain with the younger Vaughans, and, even more to the point, it also ruled out Sandy's mother; net result, no sunlit foreign holiday for the twins. Mrs Vaughan was quite immovable in her refusal to let her daughters loose on the Iberian peninsular unaccompanied, despite impassioned promises of propriety, sobriety, and any other virtue their mother might consider necessary.

Kit had been reading peacefully in her favourite corner of the garden before her sisters' invasion had shattered the tranquillity of her retreat with their pleas. She sighed and put down her book, resigned. For the time being there was obviously no likelihood of peace and quiet.

'I never cease to marvel at Mother's optimism when she named you two Charity and Clemency. You haven't a vestige of either virtue between you!' Kit hauled herself up on the lounger with an effort, the twins hastening to stack some cushions behind her.

'Not feeling funny again, Kit, are you?' Clem eyed her older sister guiltily.

'No. Just a bit feeble now and then, that's all. Another day or two and I'll be back to work.'

'Oh no, you won't,' said Charity hotly. 'Dad says you can forget about work for at least three weeks. So why not come to Spain? Think of it—ten days on the Costa del Sol, soaking up sunshine on the beach. The apartment's for free, all you have to pay for is the plane ticket, and the fares will be cheaper on October the first. Please, please, Kit! We'll do everything; you won't have to lift a finger, and Mother will be perfectly happy as long as you're with us.'

'Oh, I agree, Mother probably would. But what about me?' Kit demanded. 'A walk down the village street here in Llanhowell is more than enough with you two. And here people are used to you. The thought of your impact on the Costa del Sol is enough to give me a relapse!'

Kit's forebodings were somewhat exaggerated, but there was some justice in her objections. Charity and Clem were identical twins, mirror images of each other, with only a scar on Charity's thigh to tell them apart physically. Each had bright blue eyes, golden complexions and curling manes of ash-blonde hair, coupled with tall, spectacular figures. One of them on her own was striking; multiplied by two the effect was devastating. Katharine was six years older, with the same golden skin, but her long, thick hair was straight, and in the soft, Celtic black of her father's forebears, contrasting with eyes in a subtler, smoky blue. They looked out on the world from beneath heavy, thickly lashed lids that gave her a deceptively sleepy look completely at variance with her personality, which bordered on the astringent rather than the placid.

Deciding the time was right to help her mother with

dinner, Kit rose carefully to her feet, each twin putting
out an instinctive hand to steady her. She grinned at
them, refusing assistance, and wandered slowly towards
the house, followed dispiritedly by her sisters, their
heads together in close consultation, as usual.

Dr Harry Vaughan, his wife and four children lived in
a solid stone house built about two hundred years
before in the village of Llanhowell in the beautiful rural
area of Gwent near Monmouth. Various additions had
been added to the original building long before the days
of planning permission, with a haphazard result
attractive to the eye. The rambling structure had odd
corners with unexpected windows all looking on to the
secluded, peaceful garden that trapped whatever sun
was available all year round. In the sunny kitchen
Angharad Vaughan looked up from the pot she was
stirring and smiled at her eldest daughter.

'No need to come in yet, darling. You should have
stayed out in the sun now you're well enough to enjoy it
again.'

'I would have done, but these two shattered my
peace, so I decided to come in and make myself useful.'
Kit subsided on a ladderback chair at the kitchen table,
and grinned with malice at the disconsolate pair leaning
against one of the counter tops, eye-catching as usual in
dark blue running vests, brief striped shorts and brass-
studded leather clogs.

Mrs Vaughan nodded in resignation.

'Spain, I suppose. They've been pestering you, no
doubt. Ignore them. If you feel you must do something
you can slice these runner beans while you sit there. I've
made some tea.' She looked at her younger daughters
with disfavour. 'And you two can make yourself decent.
I would strongly advise you to get those vests in the
linen basket before Penry gets home, or he's likely to
maim you both.'

As Charity and Clem clattered obediently upstairs
Mrs Vaughan set a cup of tea in front of Kit and
handed her a bottle of small white tablets.

'Time for your Stemetil. How do you feel at the
moment?'

Kit swallowed the pill obediently and smiled cheerfully at her mother.

'Not too bad at all, really. No dizziness, no nausea, and the ground beneath my feet is actually terra firma at last instead of undulating cotton wool. What are you making?'

'Parsley sauce. I'll leave it in the double boiler until dinner time. Your father's not on call tonight and Penry will be home from his Rugby practice soon, so I thought we'd eat fairly early for once. This piece of gammon is just about at the right stage; it should be rather nice.'

'Everything you cook is "nice".' Kit sighed and went on slicing beans neatly. 'It's a pity about the twins' holiday, though, can't they postpone it until Sandy's better?'

'They'll all be back in Cardiff at college by then.' Mrs Vaughan sat down and poured herself some tea. 'Don't worry, they can go some other time.'

'I feel a bit mean,' said Kit ruefully, 'but you know what it's like, Mother. Going anywhere with them is like being part of a circus—everyone stares so much. Imagine them on a Spanish beach—they'd be a wow with the local populace; or at least the male half.'

'I don't think one gets many local people on the beach on the Costa del Sol,' murmured Mrs Vaughan, 'mostly tourists, I've heard.'

Kit looked at her parent with assessing eyes, opening her mouth to speak, but at that moment the tall figure of her young brother hurtled through the door, dumping a couple of holdalls on the floor, his face flushed and shining with sweat.

' 'Lo, Mam, Kitty-cat—what a day for rugby practice! More like cricket weather, this heat—what's to eat?'

Without waiting for an answer he opened the fridge and took out some milk, drinking most of it down in one great gulp straight from the bottle.

'Good afternoon, Penry. We do boast some of the more sophisticated accessories to gracious living, you know—like glasses and plates.' His mother sighed as

her large offspring extracted a tin from the cupboard
and wolfed down several Welshcakes without a pause.
He grinned apologetically and sat down by Kit.

'Sorry. Gruesome school lunch today—liver with
elastic bands in it, followed by rhubarb tart; yuck!
Ergo, I went without. How are you today?'

'Better, thanks. Practically normal.'

He grunted in disbelief.

'Still look a bit off to me.'

'Chatty and Clem have been working on Kit to go to
Spain now Sandy has measles,' explained his mother.
'You know how—well, persistent they can be.'

'Cripes, yes—sorry, Mam!' Penry shot an apologetic
look at his displeased parent. 'But I know what it's like.
Double trouble. Take no notice, Kit.' He got up and
thrust a hand through shaggy black hair. 'I'm off for a
shower—didn't stop for one at school. See you!'

Kit smiled as he thundered upstairs.

'We're going to find it quiet when he takes off for
college as well.'

Mrs Vaughan got up and took the colander of beans
from Kit, looking down at her whimsically.

'And what about you, Katharine? Do you intend to
stay at home for ever, or do you think it possible that
even you may fly the nest one day? It's difficult to
picture you in the role of eternal spinster, somehow.'

'I wonder why that word is so unattractive?
Furthermore, it sounds as if you want to be rid of me.
Marriage isn't statutory, you know. I've been away to
college, so you can't say I've never been from home, I
have a good job, a lot of friends, not to mention a great
set of parents who provide me with every home
comfort. So why should I yearn to leave?'

'People just do, usually.' Mrs Vaughan turned back
to the cooker. 'Not that I want to lose you, God knows,
but—well, you ought to have a man.'

Kit hooted.

'A bit basic, put like that, Mother dear. After all, I go
out with men a lot——'

'Granted; but you don't care tuppence for any of
them.'

'They're all good fun and pleasant company.' Kit stopped as her mother turned a satirical blue eye on her. 'O.K., so I haven't met Mr Right yet. Perhaps I never will, even if he exists. I imagine I'll get by just the same. I don't really think I'm the type for love well lost and all that—sounds too subservient and doormat-ish for me.'

Further discussion was cut short by the arrival of Dr Vaughan, who embraced his wife with enthusiasm and sat down near his daughter, examining her face closely. Harry Vaughan loved all his family deeply, but this, his firstborn, was the apple of his eye, with a special niche in his heart reserved solely for her.

'You really look quite good today, Kit. I think you may be out of the wood.'

'I feel great, Dad, honestly. No vertigo, nausea— nothing. I'll be back at the practice with you next week.' Kit's long blue eyes sparkled reassuringly. 'I'm sure you could do with my services.'

Dr Vaughan shook his head swiftly, meeting his wife's eye.

'The relief dispenser is doing very well. By no means as pretty, I admit, but no one's been poisoned yet, and he's very good with all your old regulars, so you relax, Katharine Vaughan. Leave your white coat on its hook for another three weeks at least, until this virus is completely out of your system. A recurrence of labyrinthitis is the last thing you want, I'm sure.'

'You can say that again,' agreed Kit fervently. 'I wish I knew how I picked the wretched virus up.'

'Could have been anywhere.' Dr Vaughan smiled up at his wife. 'Something smells good, *cariad*. What are we having?'

'Ham and parsley sauce, and all of us together for once if you get a move on. I expect Penry's out of the bath by now.' His wife smiled at him lovingly. 'Let's enjoy our meal while we have peace—I assume young Jon is doing his bit this evening.'

'That's right.' Dr Vaughan grinned at Kit. 'Sends his regards, and hopes you're not overdoing things, Kit, as per his instructions.'

'How kind. Tell him I'm following them to the letter—at least about the labyrinthitis,' Kit added with a wink.

Dr Vaughan ran a medical practice which served a far-flung rural area of Gwent. Two other doctors assisted him, and Katharine was employed as his dispenser. The younger of the two doctors, Jonathan Castle, had only recently joined the practice, and from the day of his arrival had made a dead set at Kit, much to the amusement of the various part-time receptionists who worked for her father. Jon Castle made no bones about his predilection for Kit, and even an introduction to the twins did nothing to deflect him from his aim, which was apparently to spend as much of his free time with Kit as she would allow, despite certain restrictions she firmly set on their relationship.

She was amused by Jon's undisguised enthusiasm, if completely unstirred by it, and enjoyed evenings spent in his company, at the same time making it quite clear that as far as anything deeper went he was likely to be disappointed. Undeterred, he was unfailing in his attentions, and when the unpleasant virus had struck three weeks earlier he had almost driven Kit mad with constant enquiries and gifts of every description, from flowers and books to some heavy French perfume that added considerably to her nausea.

'Poor man,' said Chatty later, as they sat enjoying succulent slices of warm ham with its complement of savoury sauce and crisp green beans with tiny potatoes. 'The trouble is, Kit, that you're so cool and discouraging. Mind you, it makes men come running all the more—terribly clever, really.'

'Not to mention terribly unintentional,' said Kit calmly.

'That's the secret,' chimed in Clem. 'You're so sort of—oblivious when men are attracted to you that they positively simmer with suppressed emotion.'

Penry looked at her with distaste.

'Don't talk such rot, Clem—puts me off my food.'

There was general laughter at such an unlikely occurrence, and the subject was changed, to Kit's relief. This was shortlived.

'I gather the girls have been pestering you to go to Spain,' said Dr Vaughan, looking at Kit. 'Might not be such a bad idea.'

There was general surprise, apart from Mrs Vaughan. Chatty and Clem gazed at their father in wonder at support from such an unexpected quarter, but Kit's eyes were dark and accusing even though she kept silent.

'Dad,' said Chatty eagerly, 'do you mean it?'

'I never dreamed you'd side with us,' agreed Clem tactlessly.

Mrs Vaughan looked at her younger daughters reprovingly.

'Your father isn't suggesting this for *your* benefit, even though that does enter into it, of course. It may have escaped your notice, but Kit has been extremely unwell for almost a month now. Your father and I agree that a quiet holiday in the sun would be a good thing for her, and as Mrs Hughes and Sandy can't go now, I suggest that Kit *and* I take their place.'

Penry gazed at his mother in horror, abandoning his mammoth portion of trifle to protest.

'What about me—and Dad?' he demanded wrathfully.

'You can both cope perfectly well for ten days, I'm sure,' said Mrs Vaughan, unmoved. 'Mrs Prosser has agreed to come in every day instead of twice a week. She will prepare some meals, I've left others in the freezer—very good practice for when you start at university. Oh, and you'll have to organise your social life so that you're in on the nights your father's on call.'

'We'll manage, don't you worry,' said Dr Vaughan reassuringly, and avoided his eldest daughter's sardonic eye. 'Should be very nice, Malaga in October—or was it Marbella?'

There was a buzz of excited chatter from the twins, but Kit was quiet, secretly appalled by the whole idea.

'Do you loathe the thought so much?' asked her mother under cover of the hubbub issuing from the rest of her family.

'You've been a bit secretive about it all,' answered Kit. 'I would have liked to be consulted first, I think.'

'In which case you'd have said no.' Mrs Vaughan rose to clear the table, summoning the twins to help. 'I'll look after these two, don't worry, and you can do exactly as you like. I gather the apartment belongs to some friends of the Hughes's and should be very pleasant, with balconies overlooking the beach and marina. You can lie there on your own all day if you like.'

When her mother spoke in a certain tone of voice Kit knew there was little more to be said, and decided her energies were best devoted to being less of a wet blanket. Perhaps she *would* enjoy it, after all. The prospect of ten days of sun was certainly alluring, unlike her holiday in the Lakes earlier in the year when it had rained quite a lot.

Kit was given little time to repine. The flights were arranged for the following week, and she turned her attention to her summer clothes. Chatty and Clem, their wish granted, were absolute angels, doing everything they could for their sister, last-minute shopping, ironing, running errands for their mother, even preparing meals.

'I might as well make the most of this burst of virtue,' said Mrs Vaughan. She and Kit were drinking coffee while the other two energetically hung out last-minute washing. 'It can't possibly last.'

'I feel I ought to be doing more to help,' said Kit idly. 'I'm really perfectly well now.'

'And we intend you to stay that way,' answered her mother forcibly. 'I know you don't care too much for the idea, so the least I can do is make sure you're not worn out before we start. The flight is late afternoon, fortunately, so Harry can drive us down comfortably to Heathrow after lunch. Jon will cope with evening surgery. A pity we couldn't get a charter flight from Rhoose, but I suppose we were lucky to manage a scheduled flight at such short notice.'

Kit looked up at the glowing, excited faces of the twins as they came running in from the garden, and her eyes softened. Both girls were so happy about their holiday she would just have to put her misgivings behind her and join in wholeheartedly with the preparations. She rose to her feet and stretched, thankful that at last it was possible to do so without any threat of vertigo.

'I think I'll sort out my bikinis, then,' she said casually, and strolled through the hall to the stairs, well aware of the beams of approbation she left behind her.

The general air of excitement prevailed in the household until the day before they were due to leave, when disaster struck. Mrs Vaughan was running downstairs with a suitcase in her hand when she missed her footing and fell heavily with an agonised cry. Her daughters ran to her from all directions, to find her in a heap at the foot of the stairs, her face paper-white as she tried to get up. Kit told her to stay where she was, leaving the twins to comfort their mother while she herself rang the practice for her father. When Dr Vaughan arrived he diagnosed a broken ankle, and Mrs Vaughan was taken off to hospital to have an X-ray, leaving Kit to comfort the upset twins. The sight of their mother's white, pain-filled face had shaken them badly, and, to be fair, it was only after they were left to themselves that realisation struck. This meant goodbye to their ill-fated holiday once again.

Kit sensibly saw to it that they were occupied with preparing the evening meal, and had the task of calming Penry when he arrived home to find that his beloved 'Mam' had had an accident. He was inclined to be accusing, considering that none of it would have happened if Mrs Vaughan had not been rushing around preparing for the holiday. In the hot argument that resulted Kit was obliged to act as referee, only the sound of their father's car quietening down the combatants as they rushed outside to welcome home a pale but determinedly cheerful Mrs Vaughan. Her husband carried her in and laid her gently on the sofa in the living room, taking care not to jar her injured leg, which was now encased in plaster.

'We've made the dinner,' said Chatty and Clem in chorus.

'Oh, my God!' said Penry in disgust. 'Then it's

bound to be out of a tin—or salad—the extent of your talents.'

'We were having salad anyway,' soothed Mrs Vaughan. 'It was very thoughtful of you to get on with it.'

'Kit's idea,' said Chatty honestly. 'To keep us occupied. How do you feel, Mother? Does it hurt horribly?'

'Not so bad now it's plastered.' Mrs Vaughan sighed ruefully. 'I'm very sorry, girls, I'm afraid I've messed things up for you.'

'Rubbish,' said Clem stoutly, 'you could hardly help breaking your ankle! We'll get to Spain another time.'

Dr Vaughan regarded the twins with surprised approval, then went through to the dining room where Kit and Penry were putting bowls of salad and coleslaw on the table. He sniffed the air appreciatively.

'What's cooking?'

'Steaks,' said Penry blissfully. 'Kitty-cat decided to give us a treat with the salad.'

His father kissed Kit's cheek as she moved past him towards the kitchen.

'Good girl,' he said fondly.

She winked saucily at him.

'My virtue knows no bounds! Come on, Pen, you bring in the jacket potatoes while I dish up the steaks.'

Mrs Vaughan insisted on sitting at table, though she ate very little and was obviously in pain, even while joking about her spectacular fall. Chatty and Clem were commendably cheerful and gay and only subsided into silence when Kit rapped her fork on her plate and demanded attention.

'Thank you! Now then, Mrs Vaughan, ma'am, do you think you can manage at home if we stick to the arrangement with Mrs Prosser? If so, I'll take the twins to Spain.'

For once the latter were dumb, staring at Kit with incredulous hope in their eyes. The other three all spoke at once.

'Of course I can manage——' began Mrs Vaughan.

'You must be mad,' said Penry gloomily.

'Well done, love,' said Dr Vaughan. 'I rather thought you would.'

'But,' said Kit firmly, as the girls came to life again, 'you two will have to behave like angels, I warn you, or I lock you up in the apartment.'

'Oh, we will, we will!' Charity and Clem threatened to smother Kit with suffocating hugs. 'We'll do anything you say—wear hats, dark glasses——'

'Nothing so extreme,' said Kit dryly, extricating herself with some difficulty. 'Just a modicum of line-toeing will do—no wild romances with waiters, or anything in that area, or I shall be worse to deal with than Mother, I assure you.' She caught her father's eye as he glanced at Mrs Vaughan. 'And now, Mother darling, I think you should allow one of these gentlemen to assist you upstairs. Chatty can help you undress while Clem and I clear up here.'

Mrs Vaughan meekly let her stalwart son pick her up with apprehensive care, and was borne off to bed to the accompaniment of innumerable instructions from husband and daughter, smiling gratefully at Kit over Penry's broad shoulder.

'Thank you, Katharine,' she said simply, leaving Kit with as much pride as if she had been awarded the Victoria Cross.

CHAPTER TWO

As the Iberia flight for Malaga took off from Terminal Two at Heathrow, Kit began to relax in her seat, thankful that the three of them were safely on board the crowded plane and this part of the journey, at least, had been achieved without a hitch. Chatty and Clem had been as good as gold so far, trying their level best to efface themselves as much as possible. Dressed carefully in an effort to avoid attention, they were both in denims and cotton shirts worn with lightweight windcheaters, their hair tied neatly back, and large sunglasses on their short, tilted noses. So far no one had given them a second look. The dinner trays had been distributed and collected again, and Kit settled down to read the paperback novel bought at the airport, the twins deep in the latest edition of *Vogue*. Eventually Charity leaned across and told Kit they were going to the loo, and would she mind if they let their hair loose, as they were a bit headachy. Kit shook her head and returned to her novel, where the heroine was plunged into a violent, explicit love scene even before page three. Marvelling at how she managed it, Kit looked up absently to find the steward asking for the money for her drink. She paid for the girls' drinks as well, privately admiring the dark, rather aristocratic Spaniard, whose long-boned saturnine good looks seemed more appropriate to a conquistador's helmet than to the airline uniform. He gave her change with grave courtesy, then she saw his eyes widen and glanced over her shoulder to see Chatty and Clem returning down the aisle blonde curls rioting about their shoulders, chattering away to each other as usual, their startlingly blue eyes animated and bright, no longer hidden by dark lenses.

Kit watched with amusement as the steward installed them in their seats across the aisle, gave unnecessary help with seatbelts and asked earnestly if there was anything they required. Obviously disappointed when they refused prettily, he went on to the next passengers, the twins smiling apologetically at Kit, who shrugged and returned to her book. There was no use in getting steamed up, they were eye-catching whatever they wore, and she might just as well resign herself to stares following them everywhere rather than let it spoil the holiday for all three of them.

They landed uneventfully in Malaga, had quite a wait before their luggage emerged on the carousel, and after they had found a taxi it was nearly eleven by the time they reached Marina Costa and the Apartamientos Teresa. Their flat was on the tenth floor, and after establishing their identity with the janitor, who spoke a little English, they were shown into a small apartment overlooking the sea. A minute kitchen and one large living-room complete with bar, two bedrooms and a bathroom constituted the entire accommodation, and Kit instructed her sisters to unpack while she made tea with tea-bags and powdered milk brought with her. The three of them were travel-weary by this time and, only pausing to make up the beds, they all tumbled into them thankfully and went off to sleep almost at once, regardless of the vibrant nightlife of the Costa del Sol, clearly audible from the street far below.

Kit woke first next morning and got out of bed yawning to look from the window at the view. She opened glass doors giving on to a small balcony and stood in the sunshine, taking in the vista of sand and sea spread out before her. To her left was a glistening white marina, brand new and still in process of completion, with boats bobbing at their moorings, looking large and expensive even from this distance. A sudden rumble in Kit's stomach reminded her that none of them had eaten since the meal on the plane the evening before, and she went next door to rouse the others so they could go out in search of breakfast. She had a quick shower while the twins came to, then went to look out a bikini, finding Chatty and Clem outside the bathroom door, still in their brief nightshirts, eyeing her uncertainly.

'What's the matter, children?' asked Kit, amused. Neither answered immediately.

'Come on,' said Kit impatiently, 'I'm starving!'

'Well,' began Chatty, 'I mean, the thing is, knowing how you feel about it—I mean, how do you want us to dress? We promised not to attract attention.'

'Too many "I means" in that,' smiled Kit, feeling suddenly extremely petty. 'I think I've been a bit "mean", too, not to mention nit-picking, about the whole thing. Put it down to the labyrinthitis—I must blame something. The only way you could stop attracting attention is to go into purdah, or take the veil. Come on, get a move on, wear what you like, only let me get near some food!'

Two radiant faces were her instant reward, as Chatty and Clem dashed off to dress, though the latter turned at the bedroom door with an ingenuous statement that left Kit rather staggered.

'Anyway, Kit, if you notice, people just use words like "stunning" and "gorgeous" about us, and half of that is because we're twins. *You* are the one they describe as beautiful.'

Kit examined herself in the mirror in her bedroom, laughing in spite of herself at the amazed expression on her face. Her long heavy hair had regained its former satiny black gloss, and her eyes sparkled from beneath the heavy lids. Her skin would soon glow again after a day or two in the sun—but beautiful? Not a word she would have applied to herself, despite Clem's touchingly sincere compliment. The twins were tall, with figures that curved in and out in spectacular fashion, but Kit was five or six inches shorter, with a trim, less arresting shape, a little inclined to the angular since her illness, but a few days' holiday would soon remedy that. Making a face at herself, she put on a hyacinth blue satinised bikini, adding white shorts and blue-striped white top, white kid thongs on her feet, finally packing a large white bag with various necessities for the beach, including the indispensable dark glasses and white floppy cricket hat with green-lined brim.

'Ready, girls?' she called, hastily making her bed.

'Ready, Kit,' they chorused, proudly indicating their tidy beds.

Kit grinned as she inspected their choice of clothes; white shorts like her own, worn with gilt sandals and some rather familiar dark blue vests.

'Does Penry know about those?' she asked as they locked up the flat.

'I expect he does by now!' Chatty giggled. 'Never mind, we'll take him back a present.'

They had breakfast at a pavement café—rolls, butter and milky coffee, consumed while they watched the passing show and incessant traffic of the Carretera de Cadiz, the main coastal highway running through the town. The twins barely gave Kit time to swallow the last mouthful before they were dragging her off the short distance to a path leading between two hotels down to the long curving balustraded terrace which ran above the sands as far as the eye could see. Suddenly Kit felt extraordinarily lighthearted as Charity and Clem hooked on to her arms on either side, and arm in arm they strolled along in the brilliant sunshine, examining the various little encampments of straw canopied mattresses, each clustering around their own small restaurant.

Deciding on a spot not too far along they made their way down a flight of steps to the sand and took possession of three of the brightly coloured mattresses nearest the sea, and within easy distance of the restaurant.

'In case we get thirsty,' said Clem happily. She and Charity stripped off shorts and vest and settled themselves on the reclining mattresses in white bikinis, busily applying suntan oil to each other while Kit disposed of her belongings more slowly, letting Charity rub in oil over her back before she settled down on the sunbed with her paperback to find out what further adventures had overtaken her tempestuous heroine.

'Kit,' said Clem a little later, 'I think the man wants some money for the chairs.'

Kit sat up and took off her glasses, looking up in

enquiry at the young man in spotless white tee-shirt and shorts who held out tickets in one hand while he frankly stared at the three girls who lay looking up at him with amused eyes of varying shades of blue. Eventually he roused himself and took the necessary money, leaving the twins chuckling shamelessly. The sunbeds near them were beginning to fill up with holidaymakers speaking in a diversity of languages. At first Kit felt apprehensive about the proximity of so many scantily clothed people, but as the mattresses were arranged in pairs, the spare one next to Kit remained unoccupied, giving her a feeling of security. As the morning wore on pop music began to sound from the restaurant's loudspeakers, British hits mingled with popular Spanish music, the blue water so near to them tempted numbers of bathers, and further out foot-operated pedalos were for hire.

The twins thought these looked great fun and tried to persuade Kit on a trip in one of the craft intended for four people.

'We'll do all the pedalling and you can just sit and enjoy the view,' they coaxed.

Kit shook her head.

'I feel too lazy. You both go, by all means, while I follow the further exploits of this witless Esmeralda in my book, and we'll have lunch when you get back.'

She watched the tall, graceful figures hurry off, aware that hers were by no means the only eyes riveted on the girls as they paid the boy in charge of the boats and clambered happily in to set off over the cobalt blue water of the Mediterranean. Kit felt quite sleepy and her eyes refused to focus on her book, so she just lay watching all the holiday activity of the beach from beneath the brim of her sun-hat. Several windsurfers were enjoying varying success on the water, and a group of small children nearby were happily engrossed in building a sandcastle, an occupation obviously just as common to Mediterranean beaches as to their counterparts in Britain.

Charity and Clem returned an hour later, bubbling over with enthusiasm for their trip and putting on Penry's blue vests to have lunch on the raised concrete platform of the restaurant. All three chose toasted sandwiches and drank the delicious *limón*, the fruity local lemonade, finishing with coffee before they returned to their mattresses for a post-prandial snooze.

'I say, Kit,' murmured Clem, as they settled down again, 'have you noticed that a lot of the females around her are topless?'

'I could hardly fail to,' said Kit dryly, 'though I can't help thinking some of them would look a whole lot more attractive if they kept their tops on!'

The twins chuckled in agreement, then subsided into silence while Kit relaxed, glad of the shade of the thatched canopy. She drifted gradually into sleep despite the music and the sounds of holidaymakers at various forms of play, forgetting any anxiety about looking after the twins and slipping away contentedly into deep slumber. She woke to anxious voices calling her name, and a hand gently shaking her.

'Kit, are you all right? You've been asleep for ages.' Charity's voice was anxious as Kit came to groggily, staring sleepily up at the two faces bent over here.

'Have I really—good lord, you should have woken me, I can't waste our holiday in sleep!' She sat up and ran her hands through her hair, smiling at the other two, who had dragged their mattresses out into the sun.

'You're supposed to be resting, after all, that's why Dad wanted you to come,' pointed out Clem. 'Now stand up and we'll pull your mattress out of the shade as well. You can do with some sun now—it's not quite so fierce.'

Kit let them fuss over her, glad of the warmth of the sun as she lay enjoying the heat while her sisters took out sketchbooks and each began to draw her own version of the jetty and the various people fishing from it. It was after five before the sun began to lose its warmth, and they decided to call it a day, wending their way back to the apartment to put on jeans and do a little necessary shopping.

They wandered around various nearby stores for an hour, busily translating prices into sterling on the little pocket calculator provided by Penry, and after

purchases of bread, butter, sugar and instant coffee,
with a couple of packets of biscuits and some very
reasonable Campari, also several cartons of orange
juice, they returned to the apartment to peruse the list
of restaurants thoughtfully provided by Sandy's
mother, complete with a small diagram of directions.
They ate dinner in a Danish/Spanish restaurant later
on, sharing a large paella between them, waiters fairly
scurrying to serve three such attractive young ladies,
and by midnight were fast asleep in bed again,
pleasantly tired by their day in the open air.

The next day passed in almost identical fashion, but
on the third day they made the acquaintance of a
Scottish family with two sons of approximately the
twins' age and two younger daughters. The McPhersons
proved a godsend. They were staying at the Hotel
Florida, not too far away from the Apartamientos
Teresa, and the boys, Angus and Bruce, hit it off with
Chatty and Clem almost immediately, taking them out
in pedalos, swimming with them, playing handball and
generally taking the onus of entertaining the twins from
Kit. The senior McPhersons were grateful to leave the
younger girls, Catriona and Elspeth, to play happily
under Kit's supervision for the odd hour while their
parents did some shopping or sightseeing. In turn,
Angus and Bruce took Charity and Clem off to a disco
after dinner each evening, leaving Kit to an early night
and a book, much to her sisters' misgivings, but to her
own secret relief.

A few days of this and Kit began to feel a great deal
livelier, and just the smallest bit bored with the beach.
Her skin had darkened to a glowing copper, a startling
background for her eyes, which shone with the lustre
of health once more, giving her a very different
appearance from the wan creature who had embarked
on the holiday with such reluctance. Two phone calls
home had reassured them about their mother's
progress, and one afternoon, while all the others were
busily engaged in various pursuits and the senior
McPhersons had returned to sit with their offspring, Kit
decided she needed a walk. Making sure the twins had a

duplicate doorkey, she told them she was off for a stroll and would see them back at the flat, took leave of the Scottish couple and wandered leisurely away in the direction of the marina.

It was something of a relief to be walking after all the lying about in the sun, and Kit settled her white floppy hat well down over her dark glasses to combat the dazzling light reflected up from the paving of the terrace. Her arms and shoulders gleamed bronze against the jade green of her sun-top and green and white striped seersucker shorts, and she drew in a deep breath in thankful appreciation of the fact that she now felt perfectly well again. Walking a little more briskly, she hefted her white towelling beach bag over her shoulder and made her way down to the marina, its brand new concrete walkways and moorings blindingly white, punctuated here and there by baby palm trees, newly planted in groups to soften the newness of the construction. Her eyes widened in admiration as she reached the moorings and wandered slowly past the various enormous yachts and cruisers secured there. Flags of many different nations fluttered from riggings that sang slightly in the breeze coming in from the sea, and Kit spent an absorbing, leisurely hour gazing at all the luxurious vessels, hazarding wildly improbable guesses at the cost of such fabulous, gleaming craft, dreaming of what it would be like to sail away in one of them on the calm blue Mediterranean waters that glittered so alluringly in the late afternoon sunlight.

Lost in her fantasising, Kit slipped slightly in a puddle of water, regaining her balance awkwardly and flushing as she realised she had an onlooker. On the deck of a graceful two-masted yacht a tall, darkly-tanned man was leaning on the handle of a mop, his teeth gleaming with appreciation in what she could see of his face. Most of it was obscured by sunglasses beneath the battered peak of an ancient denim cap that more or less matched his only other garment, faded, salt-streaked denims chopped off raggedly at the thigh. With nose in the air Kit walked swiftly away, fairly sure that the eyes behind the dark lenses were fixed on her bare back. She resisted the urge to hurry, and eventually the concrete walkway turned back at right angles towards the quay, and she was able to glance across fleetingly, irritated for some reason to find that the deck-hand, or whatever he was, had resumed his energetic deck-swabbing with unflattering promptness, leaving her rather deflated.

It was growing late and Kit began to hurry, slowing down again as she reached the quay, unable to resist looking at the half-dozen very élite and expensive-looking shops on the quayside at the end of the marina. One, a boutique, was particularly tempting, with casual expensive resort clothes arranged skillfully in its window. The name 'Milagrita' was written in flowing gilt copperplate above the door. The items that were actually priced were so expensive that after a few rough calculations Kit thought it likely the gilt could be genuine gold leaf very comfortably. She found a shop selling books and magazines a little further along, and bought a couple of bars of chocolate and a *Cosmopolitan* for the girls, running to earth an unread Georgette Heyer paperback in the international section for herself. The travel agency next door caught her eye as she passed, large placards advertising daily trips to Granada by coach, with tempting promises of tours of the Royal Chapel, the Alhambra and the Generalife Gardens, with lunch at a hotel somewhere during the proceedings. On sudden impulse she bought a ticket for next day, confident that Charity and Clem would be well supervised by the McPhersons. Kit was sure the arrangement would be agreeable to them, also the bus ticket stated time of return as six-thirty, which would bring her back well before dinner. By this time it really was late, and with only a cursory look at the tempting handbags in the next window she hurried up the curving, palm-lined causeway, arriving at the apartment to find Charity and Clem waiting for her anxiously, demanding to know where on earth she had been.

Once it was obvious that Kit had neither been carried off by white slavers nor run over by one of the buses hurtling past on the main Carretera, the girls were pleased with their gifts, and immediately enthusiastic when they heard of Kit's proposed outing, happy that she would be doing something more appealing to her taste than the less cerebral pleasures of the beach.

The only drawback was the early start. The coach was due to collect her at the foyer of the apartments just after six in the morning, and she stood at the large glass doors of the entrance, enjoying the opaline dawn colours of the sky over the sea, but shivering in the surprisingly cool air of early morning, wishing she was wearing something warmer than her short-sleeved shirt and thin pink cotton jeans. At least her toes were covered, in the pale blue sneakers decided on as suitable for the amount of walking anticipated.

The courier who came to conduct her to the Veracruz coach, parked a little farther along near the Hotel Florida, was young, dressed in white, with thick curly black hair and heavily-accented English. He told her to call him Paco and installed her in a window seat before the coach moved off to collect passengers from various hotels all the way to Torremolinos before it was full and went on its way to Malaga, to begin the tortuous slow climb up the fairly new road that wound its way through the mountains until they stopped for coffee at Rio Frio. Inside the coach sounded like the Tower of Babel, with different languages all being spoken at once, mainly American English, and at intervals Paco made an attempt to point out items of interest through his microphone. Kit's companion was an elderly lady who smiled politely, but knitted throughout the journey and made no attempt at conversation. The coach appeared to have been overbooked, and Paco's small seat alongside the driver was given up to a passenger while the courier did a precarious balancing act around the curves, hanging on to his microphone like a lifeline.

Rio Frio was some seventy kilometres from the coast, and considerably colder. Kit was glad to queue for coffee at the large roadside hostel there, not only with the passengers from her own coach, but those from five more Veracruz coaches, all apparently doing the same trip, to her surprise. The first half of the journey had been made through hillsides covered exclusively with olive groves, but after they left Rio Frio the countryside was given over to vegetables of every description, with rustling corn and the bright green of asparagus in abundance, giving way eventually to tobacco and strange perforated stone buildings which Paco announced were tobacco-drying sheds. The road itself was lined with plantations of slim, grey spindly trees, apparently a species of elm cultivated for its fast-growing properties and used for making paper.

Soon afterwards Paco pointed out a snow-capped range of mountains in the distance, the Sierra Nevada, and below them, the famous city of Granada. They disembarked near the statue of Isabella and Columbus, and were taken to the Royal Chapel to view the tombs of Isabella and Ferdinand, alongside those of Felipe and Juana La Loca, before being escorted back to the coach and driven up narrow winding streets to the great red, square-towered walls of the Alhambra. Once at the coach park of the palace, all six busloads of Veracruz tours were divided into languages; Spanish, French, German and English, and a guide allotted to each 'family', as he called it, and little lectures were given at various points through the intricately decorated lace-like mosaic interiors of the palace chambers, and the various fountain-filled courtyards much beloved of the Moors who once occupied such a large part of Spain.

Kit's head reeled, trying to remember facts and figures, but she would have enjoyed it better if only there had been fewer people there all looking at it with her. A great deal of the atmosphere was lost in the sheer density of the crowd that thronged the ancient building. She would have loved to hear more about how the Spaniards vanquished Boabdil, the Caliph who had the palace built by Christian slaves, but the tour itinerary obviously had a strict time-table and soon she was out on her way to the Generalife Gardens, where an illusion of coolness was achieved beneath the now fierce midday sun by the constant sound of running water gurgling its way down the hillside, conducted by clever Moorish canals which had diverted the snows of the Sierra

Nevada down to the warmer earth below for centuries, ensuring a never-ending water supply for the beautiful gardens and the town. After a swift tour of the gardens, brilliant with the red of geraniums against the intricate hedges of centuries-old cypress, Kit suddenly felt exhausted and giddy. She firmly clamped down on an instant feeling of panic. Telling the guide she would catch them up in the coach park in a few minutes, she sank on to a secluded rustic seat deep in the shade and hazily watched the rest of her party obediently trailing off after the guide, who was still intoning about the beauty around him as the group went out of sight.

Kit sat perfectly still, leaning her head on her arm along the back of the seat, waiting for the dreaded vertigo to subside. Oblivious to passersby, she remained quietly with eyes closed, her long black hair veiling her face, and dozed a little intermittently before coming to with a start. Glancing at her watch, she sat up in horror. She had been there an hour! Lunch would be almost over by now. She ran precipitately down the cypress-lined paths, luck rather than memory guiding her along the correct route to the large coach and car park, where, just as she had feared, there was no Veracruz coach in sight. To make things worse she had no recollection at all of the name of the hotel where lunch had been arranged for the six coach parties. Among so many people who would have been likely to miss her, she thought, panic rising inside her with a gush. She swallowed hard and tried to think calmly, marshalling her thoughts sensibly, the sole idea to occur the necessity of finding a policeman and hoping against hope he would speak enough English to understand her plight.

CHAPTER THREE

REID LIVESEY leaned morosely against the bonnet of the metallic silver Mercedes, his long legs stretched out before him as he stared at the throng of people. They were climbing into coaches, parking cars, buying icecreams and drinks, shepherding large families in all directions, everyone talking volubly at the tops of their voices; Spain, together with a great many visitors to its shores, was bent on enjoying the mid-week day of fiesta to the full.

One of the rules Reid lived by was never to act on impulse, but today he had broken it. Forgetting it was the feast day of Nuestra Señora de Pilar, he had decided to look round the tobacco growing area near Granada and make an initial investigation into the commercial potential of the region. If he had returned to the coast immediately afterwards all would have been well, but yet another impulse had prompted him to visit the Alhambra as he was in the vicinity, realising too late that owing to the holiday a great many other people had had the same idea. He lit a cheroot and watched the passing crowd, waiting for several coaches to leave before attempting to follow suit. Eventually deciding the way was clear to manoeuvre the Mercedes down the long winding exit road with reasonable ease, Reid got in the car and automatically put on sunglasses. On the point of switching on the ignition his attention was caught by the figure of a girl standing very still, oblivious of the animated people jostling her on either side. Her attention was fixed on the coach park, which by this time was deserted, without a coach in sight.

Reid hesitated. The girl was obviously Spanish. Her hair and skin were too dark for anything else. It was difficult from where he was to see much of her face, hidden as usual behind the inevitable shelter of dark glasses, but something in her stance betrayed panic.

Perhaps she was waiting for someone; possibly someone had stood her up. Either way a young Spanish lady of obviously good upbringing would probably be affronted if he accosted her, however good his intentions. He shrugged and started the car, looking back over his shoulder as he reversed carefully out of a fairly tight space. As he swung the steering wheel round he glanced fleetingly across at the girl, then heaved a resigned sigh, reversed into the space just vacated and stopped the car. The abandoned *señorita* quite obviously didn't feel well. She was leaning against a small Seat car, and if he was any judge she was about to faint. Reid swung his legs out of the Mercedes and moved like lightning, taking hold of the girl's tanned arm with apology, asking her in fluent Castilian if he could be of assistance.

'*Yo—no—hablo Español*,' gasped Kit with difficulty, '*perdone. . . .*'

The ground was heaving beneath her feet in hatefully familiar manner, and the cement-mixer in her skull had resumed its old motion. Barely aware that someone was now holding her round the waist, she fumbled ineffectually at the opening of her bag, responding instinctively to the crisp authority of the voice that now inexplicably spoke English, asking her what she wanted.

'My pills,' she panted. 'In—my bag, somewhere.'

Reid Livesey frowned.

'Pills?'

'Stemetil—if you could just unscrew the bottle.'

He searched through a variety of feminine clutter, located the bottle, shook one out into her unsteady palm and looked down at her in enquiry.

'Can you swallow it dry?'

'Have to.' Kit gulped determinedly, by now aware of the arm about her waist, but unwilling to look up at her rescuer. 'I'm sorry to be a nuisance.'

'Don't apologise. It might be an idea if you sit in my car for a while until you feel more the thing.'

Kit allowed herself to be guided the short distance to the long silver car, each step an experiment as to the stability of the ground beneath her feet. She sighed with relief as she sank into the car's soft leather seat, the immediate feeling of security doing wonders for her errant equilibrium. As her rescuer opened the door on the other side of the car Kit removed her sunglasses to look properly at her good samaritan for the first time. As the man folded himself neatly into the low driving seat her first startled impression was that he was all one colour, hair and skin the same red-brown. He removed his own glasses to look at her and she saw that his eyes were light, a clear hazel that was almost yellow. Like a fox, she thought, then blushed as she realised she was staring.

'That's better,' he said approvingly. 'More colour in your face. Do you feel less faint now?'

'I wasn't precisely faint before,' she said apologetically. 'I've been ill, with labyrinthitis, and——'

'What in God's name is that?' His teeth gleamed white in his dark face, and Kit frowned slightly. Had she met him before, or was it just a case of déjà-vu? He seemed definitely familiar. She smiled faintly.

'Just a virus. Makes one feel permanently seasick, though I really thought I was completely recovered; I'm in Spain to convalesce, actually.' Her face suddenly blanched and she looked across the car park wildly. 'I'd forgotten—I came here by coach and it's gone without me. I was just looking round for a policeman when——'

'I saw you about to fold up and risked offending a high-born Spanish *señorita* by grabbing you.' Reid was purposely flippant in an effort to calm her. My God, he thought, all of Spain to choose from and I land myself with a stranded tourist!

'You were very kind.' Kit recollected herself hurriedly. 'Thank you very much, Mr——?'

'Livesey. Reid Livesey.'

'Katharine Vaughan.'

'Well, Miss Katharine Vaughan, what are we going to do about you? Where are you supposed to be at this precise moment? And at the risk of appearing rude, how did you become separated from your party?'

The searching, light eyes turned on her made Katharine feel slightly chilled. This man's casually efficient rescue had been kind, but impersonal in the extreme, almost verging on boredom.

'I think I should be having lunch, in the company of six coach-loads of tourists, at a hotel whose name escapes me, unfortunately,' she began, thinking it best to let him know the worst. 'The only thing I can think of is to ring the travel agency where I bought the ticket and ask them if they know the Veracruz coaches' itinerary and then take a taxi to wherever the coach is at the moment, presumably waiting near the hotel where the lunch is arranged.'

With a look on his face Kit could only describe as resigned, Reid Livesey held out a long, well-cared-for hand for her coach ticket, which was in a folder similar to those issued by airlines.

'Good. The telephone number's on the folder,' he said briefly. 'I'll do the telephoning—I gather your Spanish is hardly up to it?'

Kit shook her head, instantly regretting it, then took out a thousand-peseta note from her purse. She held it out to the man, who looked down at the note with all the distaste he would have accorded an obscene postcard.

'Unnecessary,' he said shortly, and got out of the car before she could argue further.

Kit watched him walk away with mixed feelings. Taller than he looked sitting down, he was lean and muscular rather than massive, and walked with a collected, self-contained economy of movement. His perfectly cut cream poplin trousers and matching tussore shirt fitted him like bespoke garments, if the term were still used, she mused idly, and altogether he exuded an air of money and authority, all the more effective for its very understatement. She watched as he paused to speak to an attendant, a reddish glint in his hair catching the sun. It was very thick hair, cut close to lie against his head like the pelt of an animal. Kit smiled faintly; back to the fox again—presumably better than a wolf! Her eyes drooped in the heat of the stationary car while she tried to calm her worried mind. How stupid it had been to come on a trip like this alone, or at least until she was completely over this wretched viral thing that seemed to keep coming back when least expected, or wanted. Thank heavens the rather distant Mr Livesey had been on hand when the car park had begun to revolve in sickening slow motion—Kit sighed, then jerked upright as the car door opened and her involuntary rescuer seated himself behind the wheel.

'Did you get through?' she asked anxiously.

'No. There was no answer.' He turned in his seat to look at her, unsmiling. 'Either it was still siesta time or, what's more likely, they're closed. It's a public holiday.'

Kit took a deep breath.

'Is—is there public transport I can use? Train, bus, anything?' she asked without much hope. She rubbed a clenched fist against her forehead. 'I should never have left the twins!'

'Twins?' Reid Livesey stiffened, his composure shaken for the first time. His eyes dropped automatically to her left hand. 'Are you married?'

'If the twins were mine no doubt that would have been by far the best arrangement!' Kit looked him in the eye for the first time, her worried expression replaced for a moment by a smile that curved her lips away from even white teeth and lit a spark of humour in her troubled blue eyes. 'They're my younger sisters, actually, and I'm in Spain with them in loco parentis— in place of my mother. She broke her ankle or she would be here too.' The smile vanished. 'I apologise for being so boringly awkward, Mr Livesey, but have you any suggestions as to the best way to get back down to the Costa del Sol? We're staying near Marbella, at Marina Costa, and if I don't get back in good time Charity and Clem are likely to be frantic.'

Reid looked at her expressionlessly for a moment, then started the engine.

'I'll take you.'

The luxurious vehicle glided noiselessly away towards the exit. Katharine swallowed convulsively.

'But, Mr Livesey, you can't do that——'

'Why not?' A casual glance from cool hazel eyes was dismissive.

'But it's hours away, then you'd have a return trip, and already it's mid-afternoon. I really can't permit you——'

'There's no question of permission, Miss Vaughan.' The superiority of his tone made the hairs of Kit's spine stand on end. 'Even if there *is* public transport available—and frankly I don't care to exert myself to find out—you're very obviously not well enough to travel alone. Incidentally, do you feel better now?'

'Physically, yes,' said Kit quietly.

'Good.'

They continued the twisting descent into Granada in silence, and were through the town and on the main highway heading towards Malaga before he spoke again.

'If it makes you feel any better, Miss Vaughan,' he said, keeping his eyes on the road, 'I'm staying in Marina Costa myself, so it really is very little trouble to give you a lift.'

Kit breathed in deeply.

'Then why on earth didn't you say——' she stopped short as the reason occurred to her. 'Of course—how obtuse of me! There's always the possibility of running into each other again in Marina Costa, and I might be the type to presume on our acquaintance.' She cast a hostile glance at her rescuer's unperturbed profile.

'Not in the least. I didn't realise where the phone number was until I reached the telephone booth, and when I returned to the car you rather threw me with your remark about twins.'

Kit subsided, regretting her outburst. After all, the man was getting her out of an awkward situation. She would just have to put a good face on it and behave as her mother would expect in the circumstances. Looking up uncertainly at the uncompromising profile, she smiled as sweetly as she could, and set out to be as polite and appreciative as possible.

'I had so much wanted to visit the Alhambra,' she told him, 'but I just never expected such a big crowd there, especially at this time of the year. I would have liked more time to look at the wonderful lace-like decoration, and to linger for a while in the various courtyards and listen to the tinkle of the fountains, especially the unique one with the lions.'

Reid's face relaxed a little.

'Apparently more than forty million people visit the Alhambra each year.'

'I can well believe it,' agreed Kit fervently. 'It felt as though quite a lot of them were there today.'

He grinned for the first time.

'You chose a double holiday. Apart from the religious festival this is the anniversary of the day Christopher Columbus sailed the ocean blue and discovered America.'

'Which explains a lot! By the time I reached the Generalife gardens I just had to have a rest, so I told the guide I'd catch up and found myself a secluded seat in the shade. It proved to be a bit too secluded, as the next thing I knew it was an hour later. What an idiot I am!' Kit sighed in disgust.

'Don't worry about it any more,' Reid advised coolly. 'You'll arrive home safely, and some time earlier, by your present mode of transport. But if you'll take a word of advice—well meant, I assure you—don't go wandering too far on your own for the rest of your holiday.'

'Don't worry,' Kit assured him. 'I shall stick to the beach and leave forays into culture to other people.' She gave him a wicked little smile. 'And I promise on my honour that if I see you anywhere I'll just give a polite smile and pass by without a word.'

'Oh, I hope not,' he said easily. 'Besides, I'm fairly sure we've encountered each other already.'

Kit's eyebrows rose.

'I don't think so—unless you've seen me on the beach?'

'Didn't you stroll along the marina yesterday evening? You slipped just as you passed the ketch.' He grinned at her look of astonishment.

'You were the man with the mop?' Kit eyed him critically. 'You look a bit different today.'

'Of course. I don't go in for fancy gear to swab a deck.'

She was thoughtful for a moment.

'How did you recognise me?' she asked curiously. 'My hair was pushed up under my sunhat and I had dark glasses on. The same as you, really. You look very different as you are now.'

'Oh, I didn't recognise *you*, Miss Vaughan,' he said deflatingly. 'You have a large metal initial K on your bag. The sun struck on it yesterday, and it was the first thing I noticed when you asked me to find your pills.'

'So you knew all the time where I'd come from,' Kit said quietly.

'Yes, I did.'

'You didn't offer a lift immediately.'

'You might have had a muscular husband waiting somewhere for you, also it's not a characteristic of mine to act on impulse.'

Kit turned long, deceptively lazy eyes in his direction.

'It must make life very dull for you,' she said sweetly.

'Not dull. Orderly is a better word.'

After that Kit felt little inclination to talk, apart from an occasional polite comment on some particularly spectacular part of the route, and was thankful when they arrived back in Marina Costa. Ried Livesey brought the car to a halt in a parking space in front of the Apartamientos Teresa, and turned to look at Kit.

'Safe and sound, Miss Vaughan.'

Kit smiled politely.

'You've been very kind, Mr Livesey; I can't stress too much how grateful I am. Goodbye.' She opened the door, but he put out a hand and caught her wrist. Kit turned back in surprise, meeting his impersonal gaze with a look of enquiry. He removed his hand instantly.

'I merely wished to repeat my advice. Don't venture too far alone again. Next time you might not be so fortunate.'

'I'm well aware of that. Thank you again. Goodbye.' Kit was out of the car swiftly and walked away briskly without looking back, intent on getting away at speed. Wretched man! Without him her situation in Granada could have been very awkward, she well knew, but something in his detached, superior attitude made her hackles rise. She felt utterly irritated instead of suitably grateful.

Charity and Clem had only arrived back from the beach minutes before Kit let herself in, and were surprised to see her back so early. With some misgivings she gave them a much watered-down version of her little adventure, playing down her dizzy spell and concentrating on her rescuer.

'Was he young and good-looking, Kit?' asked Chatty excitedly. 'How thrilling!'

'It wasn't the least bit thrilling at the time,' said Kit prosaically. 'One of the more idiotic things I've managed to do in my life.'

'Yes, but was he attractive?' persisted Clem.

'Not bad—a bit supercilious, actually, and quite aggravating when it came to telling me not to do it again, as if I were a naughty little girl.'

'What a hoot!' Chatty looked at Kit eagerly. 'What does he do—is he on holiday? Where's he staying? Was it a gorgeous car?'

Kit flopped down on the cushions of the small cane settee, glad to relax in the cooler evening air coming through the verandah doors.

'The car is a silver-grey Mercedes, very nice indeed, but I didn't enquire as to Mr Livesey's personal dossier, and he certainly didn't volunteer anything. Once he knew where I was staying it was obvious he was concerned that I might presume upon the acquaintance, as it were, should we happen to meet again by chance. Message noted and received, over and out.'

'Oh, Kit!' Clem looked at her older sister in despair. 'I suppose you went all remote and uninterested, as usual.'

'Not a bit of it! The boot was more on the other foot this time.' Kit hesitated. 'Actually, the strange thing was that we *had* actually seen each other before—last night.' She laughed as the twins turned identical looks of surprise on her. 'He was mopping up the deck of a very expensive-looking yacht, a ketch, I think he called it, when I was wandering round the marina, so it beats me what he was doing in Granada, he didn't strike me as keen on doing the tourist bit.' Her face darkened. 'And now I suppose I must avoid the marina like the plague, in case he thinks I'm trying to see him again. Damn!'

'But you promised to show us the dress shop you saw,' said Chatty plaintively.

'Well, I suppose I could do that. We're hardly to run into him there. Now then, my little darlings, do you think I could persuade you to make me a cup of tea and a piece of toast? I've had nothing to eat all day, apart from coffee, and I'm just about expiring from malnutrition!'

With extravagant apologies Chatty and Clem sprang into action and provided Kit with a tea-tray at top speed.

'Don't eat too much, though,' advised Clem. 'The McPhersons have asked us to their hotel for the dinner dance tonight and they want us to be their guests.'

'That's very kind of them, but I feel a bit done in——' began Kit dubiously.

'Oh, please come, Kit,' begged Chatty. 'It's only just gone six. You can have a lie down for a couple of hours, then a bath, and you'll feel a lot better. Bruce and Angus are coming to collect us at nine, so there's plenty of time.'

Kit already felt a good deal better after the reviving tea, and the welcome toast. She grinned at the two pleading faces.

'O.K. I'll have an hour or so on my bed with the voluptuous Esmeralda, which is where she spends most of the time in the book, and by then you two can have had your baths and give me time to have a soak.'

By the time the McPherson boys came to collect them later that evening, Kit was feeling remarkably lively, considering her eventful day. Her rest had done wonders and she was quite pleased with her appearance. After some coaxing from her sisters she was wearing a dress unworn until now for lack of the right occasion. A deceptively simple sheath of heavy coral-red taffeta, it left one shoulder bare before skimming past her waist

to an asymmetrical hem. Her hair shone rewardingly
after a swift shampoo and her sun-flushed face needed
very little make-up apart from eyeshadow and a rather
brighter lipstick than usual, to produce a result that was
very gratifying. The twins were very complimentary.

'About time you finally wore that dress, Kit—
fabulous with your tan. Will we do?' Charity looked
anxious. 'We bought our dresses in a summer sale, do
you think they're suitable?'

The twins looked ravishing in white broderie anglaise
dresses with flounced skirts, and Kit lost no time in
telling them so.

'You don't think these red sandals look a bit much
on me?' asked Clem, frowning, 'but if I wear white like
Chatty no one will know who's who.'

'Neither of you ever fools me.' Kit smiled indulgently.
'And yes, I think the red looks good, apart from
avoiding confusion.'

Confused was hardly the word for Bruce and Angus
when they rang the doorbell promptly at nine. They
looked stunned at the picture presented by Kit in her
red flanked by a twin in white on either side.

Earnestly instructing all three girls to stay close
during the short walk to their hotel, making extravagant
prophecies about fighting off competition of all
nationalities, the boys kept up a barrage of nonsense
until they joined the other McPhersons at their dinner
table on the edge of the small dance floor, where a
small group played disco music to the accompaniment
of the multilingual chatter of the elegantly dressed
crowd of diners in festive mood.

Chatty and Clem glittered with excitement as Mr and
Mrs McPherson teased them goodnaturedly about the
attention they were attracting. Their evenings had been
very enjoyable up to now, but this was more
sophisticated, more in keeping with their idea of a
glamorous holiday. Kit smiled at them affectionately as
they chattered away happily to the boys and watched
the dancers, hardly aware of the delicious dinner they
were eating. She turned to the McPhersons and began
to give them an amusing account of her eventful trip to

Granada while she ate her steak in pepper sauce and enjoyed the red wine provided in abundance.

Morag McPherson was half amused, half appalled.

'How fortunate you were to be rescued.'

Kit pulled a face.

'My rescuer wasn't exactly overjoyed with the whole thing—but obviously a man of conscience who couldn't ignore a damsel in distress!'

'Thank God he didn't,' said Alec McPherson fervently. 'What would you have done otherwise?'

'I was just praying for a linguistic policeman, when I was provided with the rather austere Mr Livesey instead,' said Kit lightly. 'Though, to be fair, he did all that could have been expected—even to the point of grave admonishings about my not wandering so far afield alone in future. And after all, at worst, it would just have meant blowing all my spare pesetas on a taxi.'

The McPhersons were obviously affected by her account, however, and told her to stay closer at hand in future, though making it clear that keeping an eye on the twins had been no trouble whatsoever.

'Once one recovers from the first visual impact,' said Morag wryly, 'they really are very nice lassies—a shame your mother couldn't come.'

Kit heartily agreed, and thanked her hosts sincerely for taking care of Charity and Clem and for the evening's entertainment. They watched with amusement as the four younger ones gyrated on the dance floor, the twins moving in perfect unison, no matter how far away from each other, serenely ignoring the attention they attracted from every male eye in the room.

The tempo of the music changed to something Alec McPherson felt able to cope with and he insisted on Kit dancing with him while his wife went up to check on their small daughters. As they moved leisurely round the room Kit told her partner more about the beauty of the Alhambra, her face animated as she described the Moorish architecture. Smiling up at the genial Scot, her gaze wandered a little past his stalwart shoulder, held by the look in a pair of eyes whose narrowed gaze was familiar. Reid Livesey was seated at a table some way back from the dance floor. The fleeting moment of recognition was lost as the music stopped and Alec McPherson guided Kit across the crowded floor back to their table, where Mrs McPherson was settling an amicable argument between her sons and the twins as Kit sat down.

'Bruce and Angus think they can tell us apart now,' Chatty's eyes danced at Kit, 'even if my scar is covered up.'

Kit smiled absently, inwardly quite put out by Reid Livesey's presence, and reassured the two young men.

'People do get confused by them,' she warned goodnaturedly. 'They never fool me, though.'

'We'll wear jeans down to the beach in the morning.' Clem's face was alight with mischief. 'Then you can put your theory to the test—you can buy us icecreams if you lose.'

'Right—you're on!' Bruce looked at her speculatively. 'And what if we win?'

'We'll buy *you* icecreams, of course,' said Chatty firmly, before either young hopeful could make any other suggestion.

There was general laughter at the disappointed expressions on the boys' faces, and Kit picked up her small gilt purse, excusing herself to find the powder room and make some necessary repairs. She examined her flushed face critically in the brightly lit mirror of the luxurious ladies' room, but a little more lip-gloss was obviously the only repair work necessary. Anything less like a convalescent was hard to imagine, she thought ruefully, scowling at her radiant reflection. She pulled a comb unnecessarily through her hair, tweaked her dress into place and returned through the hotel foyer towards the ballroom. She experienced a sinking feeling in her stomach when she recognised the tall, slim figure in a lightweight beige suit standing between her and her goal.

'Good evening, Miss Vaughan,' said Reid Livesey, giving her an appraising look from top to toe. 'You appear to have made a miraculous recovery.'

'Due to your kind offices, mainly, Mr Livesey,'

countered Kit evenly. 'With the added benefit of some British tea and a couple of hours' sleep. I hadn't expected to meet you again, especially so soon, but I'm glad of the opportunity to reiterate my thanks.'

'You know where the *Golondrina* is moored,' he said, one eyebrow raised.

'I rather felt you would prefer me to avoid the marina from now on,' said Kit, unsmiling. 'I thought it was agreed I shouldn't try to foist myself on you in the unlikely event of our meeting again.'

'I don't remember agreeing to any such thing. You were the one who said that, not I!' He smiled at her, with a sudden warmth in the yellow eyes transforming his expression completely.

'Shall we say you didn't trouble to deny it.' Kit was impatient, looking over his shoulder pointedly towards the ballroom. 'Now, if you'll excuse me, I must rejoin my sisters and our hosts.'

'I noticed your beautiful twins,' he murmured, standing his ground as she made to pass.

Kit threw him a sardonic look.

'Most people do. Goodbye, Mr Livesey.'

'Why goodbye? I was hoping you would dance with me.'

She looked up suspiciously into the intent eyes, then slowly shook her head.

'I'll sit this one out, Mr Livesey, if you don't mind. My father would consider I've had more than enough excitement for one day.'

He still stood in her way, smiling down at her faintly.

'Do you always concede to parental bidding, Miss Vaughan, even though—I hesitate to offend—you're not precisely a teenager?'

'I was referring to his professional opinion, actually.' Kit gave him a small saccharine smile. 'He's a doctor. Now I really—oh dear!'

Charity and Clem were hovering in the doorway, their faces anxious.

'Where have you been, Kit? We were worried—not feeling funny, are you?' They looked at her companion with frank interest.

'No.' Kit sighed. 'In fact you might say my sense of humour was having the evening off.' Bitterly aware that Reid's mouth was twitching, she introduced him to her sisters.

'Mr Reid Livesey, girls, my kind rescuer in Granada. Mr Livesey, my sisters, Charity, Clemency.'

Resigned, Kit watched as the twins poured out their gratitude to the amused man, two pairs of large blue eyes fixed on his face as they told him how ill Kit had been, and how difficult it would have been if he had not been there to bring her home.

'I'm sure someone would have helped out,' he said eventually, looking very directly at Kit, bringing the colour to her cheeks. 'Though tonight anything less like a languishing invalid is hard to picture.'

Kit's colour deepened as the twins looked from her to the tall, elegant man, their eyes sparkling, obviously scenting what they hoped was a promising situation.

'We must rejoin the McPhersons, girls——' she began, but Reid Livesey interrupted smoothly.

'I'm sure your sisters will excuse you for the space of one dance with me, Miss Vaughan.'

The twins' assent was embarrassingly enthusiastic, and willy-nilly Kit found herself on the small floor in Reid Livesey's arms. To her annoyance the group was playing Latin-American music instead of the disco beat of earlier on, and the dancers on the crowded floor were moving slowly to the lazy, more intimate rhythm, closely pressed together under dimmed lights. There was little space to move at all very much, but her partner held Kit quite impersonally, taking no advantage of their enforced proximity. After only a minute or two the music stopped, and Kit breathed a sigh of relief, then looked up sharply as she realised Reid was guiding her in the wrong direction.

'I would like you to meet some friends of mine,' he said pleasantly, holding her arm so firmly that Kit had little choice but to go where he led, which was to the table where she had seen him sitting earlier. It was now occupied by two young men who were eyeing their progress with keen interest. Both of them sprang to their feet as Reid introduced Kit to them.

'La Señorita Katharine Vaughan,' he said formally. 'May I present Luis and Carlos Santana, friends of mine.'

Each young man bowed over Kit's hand, raising it to within a fraction of their lips, smiling at her with unconcealed admiration. They both spoke fluent, slightly accented English and pressed her to sit down, snapping peremptory fingers for a waiter, who materialised instantly. Reid smiled as Kit refused anything alcoholic.

'I've had a glass of red wine with dinner,' she said apologetically, 'and I really don't think I should indulge any further.'

'Ah, but Miss Vaughan,' said Carlos Santana, 'just a glass of Sangria, this would not be harmful, I promise. You like our Sangria?'

When Kit admitted she had not tasted it a tall glass jug of the mixture, afloat with orange slices and ice cubes, appeared like magic. Finding its taste quite innocuous, she sipped cautiously at first, then with increasing assurance as she answered questions from the two young men, cousins apparently. They were surprisingly grey-eyed, with quite light brown hair, contrasting effectively with their deeply tanned skins. Both were dressed in well cut off-white suits, and Kit noted absently that their ties were pure silk, matching their shirts. Luis was a year or two older than Carlos, and more heavily built, but otherwise they looked more like brothers than cousins.

'I expected all Spaniards to be dark,' said Kit, smiling from one to the other.

'But then,' said Luis, 'one thinks of all ladies from Inglaterra as fair—the English rose—and you are as dark as any Spanish *señorita*. Am I not right, Reid? Do you not think Miss Vaughan looks very Latin?'

'But for the blue eyes,' said Reid shortly, sounding bored.

'But then,' said Kit quickly, 'I am not an English rose, as you put it, Señor Santana. My home is in Wales, though I admit our national emblem doesn't suit me either. I'm hardly the daffodil type, unlike my sisters.'

'You have many sisters?' asked Carlos.

'Just two.' Kit smiled. 'No doubt you've noticed them on the dance floor, the tall fair twins in white—they rarely go unnoticed!'

'*Es verdad!*' said Luis emphatically, his eyes following where Kit indicated, 'they are very beautiful indeed, we saw them earlier.'

'Your parents are fortunate to possess daughters of so much beauty,' said Carlos gallantly, 'do you have brothers also?'

'Just one, the baby of the family. He's eighteen, and the clever one.' Kit shook her head firmly as Reid proffered the jug of Sangria. 'No, thank you, I think I'll stop while I'm ahead.'

Reid looked at her mockingly, leaning forward to say almost inaudibly.

'Presumably you don't wish to repeat this afternoon's experience!'

She was nettled.

'Which experience do you mean, Mr Livesey? The trip to Granada was very pleasant, it was only the rest of the day's events I'd rather forget.'

His eyes grew cold, and he was obviously about to say something cutting when Luis turned to Kit from his contemplation of her sisters, who were both together with the McPherson boys in the middle of the floor indulging in some fairly energetic movement to the latest disco hit.

'What is the name of your sister—the one in the white slippers?'

Kit looked at him in surprise.

'Charity,' she said, 'and the other is Clemency.'

'Miss Charity is older than her sister?' Luis's eyes were following Chatty's graceful movements as he spoke.

'Only by about ten minutes or so,' said Kit, amused. 'Why do you think she looks older?'

Carlos laughed openly at his cousin.

'I did not even notice the different shoes—to me both young ladies seem to be identical.'

Luis shook his head, ignoring his cousin's amusement.

'Not if one looks long enough.'

Reid rose abruptly to his feet.

'I'm sure Miss Vaughan would like to rejoin them now,' he said, frowning at the Santana cousins.

Kit got up instantly, feeling offended, and despite the protests of the young Spaniards, bade them both farewell, with polite thanks for her barely touched drink before allowing herself to be led across the floor towards the McPhersons' table, Reid's hand holding her elbow in a grasp which felt like a police escort.

'Miss Vaughan, I should like to explain——' Reid said quietly as they paused to avoid a group of dancers.

'Please don't, Mr Livesey.' Kit addressed herself icily to the knot of his white-dotted brown foulard tie, her colour high. 'You've made yourself crystal clear without saying a word. If you'll release my arm I'll leave you here—saving you any more unwanted introductions.'

Reid merely tightened his grip and compelled her to move with him to the door leading into the foyer. Kit had no choice but to follow him into the deserted reception hall, where he unceremoniously pushed her down on to a small velvet settee, seating himself at right angles to her so that it was difficult for her to escape.

She glared up into the distant amber eyes so close to hers, at a loss to explain why she felt so furious.

'Now,' he said forcibly, 'if you'll keep quiet for a moment I was just about to say that I danced with you because the Santanas very much wanted an introduction.'

Speechless, Kit stared up at his dark face wrathfully.

'Otherwise, of course, you would never have acknowledged my unwanted presence here at all!'

'No, of course not,' he said impatiently, frowning. 'What I was trying to explain——'

'There's no need to say anything further!' exploded Kit, pushing him aside and jumping to her feet. 'I have no idea why the other two young men wanted an introduction——'

Reid stood blocking her way.

'If you'll just let me finish——'

'No. If you're just warning me not to speak to strange men in future, don't exert yourself. I shall avoid doing so at all costs—from this moment on!'

For a long moment they stood staring implacably at each other, the colour running high along Kit's cheekbones, then abruptly,

'Stupid girl,' Reid muttered, and seizing her upper arms in a grip likely to leave fingerprints he kissed her resentful mouth hard. Kit stayed still for the space of one surprised moment, then wrenched herself free, breathing hard, giving him one annihilating look before turning on her heel and returning to the ballroom.

Kit rejoined the McPhersons at their table just as Charity and Clem were coming off the dance floor with the boys, and resigned herself to a barrage of questions from everyone, including the senior McPersons, who were highly amused at the signs of fury Kit was doing her best to hide.

'Mr Livesey—or do you call him Reid——' said Clem eagerly.

'I don't call him anything,' said Kit flatly, privately thinking there were a number of things she could call him that might shock her present company.

'But he asked you to dance, Kit,' said Chatty, 'so he must have wanted to follow up your meeting.'

'He danced with me in almost total silence for all of two minutes, then took me over to his table where he introduced me to his friends, two Spanish cousins, Carlos and Luis Santana. I hadn't exhanged more than a couple of sentences with them before he more or less physically hauled me away again, saying it was time to get back to you.' Kit's face was stony as she furtively examined her arms, surprised that they showed no marks from her recent encounter.

'You should have brought him over to the table and introduced him,' said Morag McPherson slyly. 'He looked very interesting from where I was.'

'I'd had more than enough of him for one day,' said Kit irritably, then looked repentantly at her hostess. 'Sorry to be rude, but he rather rubs me up the wrong way.'

'You looked ready to have a punch-up as you left the room, but the girls wouldn't let us join in,' said Bruce, grinning from ear to ear.

'For which I'm profoundly grateful,' said Kit with asperity, then smiled reluctantly as she saw everyone was trying hard not to laugh.

'He's really rather gorgeous, Kit,' Clem said wistfully. 'Couldn't you have been a bit more friendly? I mean, he did rescue you and all that.'

'He didn't exactly have to slay a dragon, or anything!' By this time Kit was becoming rapidly fed up with the whole thing. 'The wretched man merely gave me a lift. Presumably any reasonable person would have done the same.'

'Leave the lassie alone,' interrupted Alec McPherson kindly, frowning at his sons. 'Now how about another drink, Kit, to cool you down?'

Kit gratefully accepted a tonic water, and soon afterwards the party broke up to her relief. Their table was not far from the exit, and they were able to make their departure without encountering Reid and his companions. Kit was glad to leave, her enjoyment of the evening spoiled by her encounter with the aloof Mr Livesey. The not-so-aloof kiss was something she put out of her mind firmly as the McPherson boys walked them back to the apartment building, though she was unable to prevent herself wondering why on earth the maddening man had sought her out to dance apparently solely on his young friends' urging. He obviously found her company boring, and having made the desired introduction seemed unwilling to let her talk to the charming Santana cousins. In which case why go to the bother of introducing her to them in the first place? Kit gave up, thanking Bruce and Angus as they took their leave, and ascending in the lift to the expected accompaniment of curious questions from Charity and Clem about the Santanas.

'We saw you at their table when we were dancing,' said Clem. 'Very nice indeed, Kit. Do they live locally? Are you going to see them again——'

Kit held up a hand for silence as she unlocked the

door to the flat, flopping wearily on the sofa and accepting offers of tea gratefully.

'They're cousins by the name of Santana, I don't know where they live, and no, I am not going to see any of them again, especially Mr Reid Livesey—at least, not if I see him first!' She stared moodily down at her gilt sandals, while her sisters exchanged rather thoughtful glances.

'Perhaps you ought to change into your nightie,' said Clem. 'Pity to crease that dress. I'll hang it up for you.'

Surprised, Kit allowed herself to be waited on, and eventually returned to the small sitting-room for the promised cup of tea and the chat the twins were obviously looking forward to. The girls had both changed into brief night-shirts and cleaned off their make-up, giving such an impression of youthful innocence as they sat on the floor side by side, drinking from thick white mugs that Kit's ill-humour dissipated.

'You two look too good to be true,' she said indulgently. 'Sometimes I wonder if that look of innocence is genuine.'

Charity gave her a wicked grin.

'Innocence and ignorance, Katharine, are two different things. And in any case, up to now we like to do things together——'

'Which members of the opposite sex find restricting,' added Clem. 'So we stick to a group in college, and avoid specific dates usually.'

'No time, anyway,' said Chatty gloomily. 'We're generally rushing to finish work on our portfolios; fabrics this term—not to mention trying to get chunks of Art History into our little brains.'

'Besides,' Clem went on, 'two of us at once seems a bit much for a lot of men.'

'Why don't you start wearing different clothes?' suggested Kit. 'Concentrate on being just sisters now that the initial impact on Cardiff has been made. Have different hairdos and develop your own individual personalities. I know very well that you're both quite different in a great many ways. Cultivate separate interests, function unilaterally for a change.'

The younger girls were silent for a while, then they looked at each other doubtfully.

'I suppose so——' they said simultaneously, then began to giggle as Kit laughed, shaking her head.

'You'll never stop doing that, I suppose—nor would we want you to.'

'Did you change the subject so that we'd lay off the fascinating Mr L., not to mention the sexy Spaniards?' demanded Chatty suspiciously.

Kit rose to her feet, yawning.

'Not entirely—but it's a great idea now you come to mention it. I'm fed up to my little molars with the man.'

'I still think you should have been more friendly with him,' persisted Clem. 'I know you're choosy, but what more could you want? He's madly elegant, attractive, gorgeous red hair—I like the way it's cut close to his head without being too short; just touching the collar at the back of his neck.'

'I didn't notice,' said Kit, with superb indifference. 'And his hair isn't really red, it's a much more subtle colour.'

Ignoring the wicked smiles of her sisters at her last remark, she bade them a lofty goodnight and went to bed.

CHAPTER FOUR

THE noonday sun was hot. Kit lay on her stomach on the sunbed, thinking idly that it was nearly time to push it back in the shade of the thatched canopy. The twins lay somnolent alongside her in the same position, motionless for once, glad to lie still and do nothing like Kit, who was enjoying the rest after the hectic adventures of the day before, followed by the equally eventful evening. Eventually the heat prodded her into moving and she got up to push the heavy wooden frame of the beach-bed under the shade.

'Allow me, Señorita Vaughan.'

Kit straightened sharply, turning in surprise to see the Santana cousins, both dressed casually in brief shorts and shirts left unbuttoned over broad tanned chests.

'Good morning—or I suppose I should say good afternoon,' she said, smiling warmly as Luis Santana pushed the mattress back under the canopy with one negligent heave.

Charity and Clem rolled over immediately and sat up to look at the two men, smiling shyly at the undisguised admiration in the unexpectedly light eyes of the cousins.

'My sisters, Charity and Clemency Vaughan,' said Kit hurriedly. 'Señores Luis and Carlos Santana.'

There was a flurry of pleasantries, much heaving and placing of the twins' sunbeds, and the two young men soon put the girls at ease with questions about their holiday, which brought forth sincerely glowing comments from the twins, who were revelling in their first trip to Spain.

Kit looked on, feeling like a duenna as she watched the two smiling animated faces blossom under the attention from the charming Spaniards. To her approval the girls had acted on last night's suggestion, and today were dressed differently, Chatty in a bright blue bikini with her hair tied up in one great mass of curls on one side of her head, and Clem in white, her hair tied at the nape of her neck with a scarlet and white scarf. Thank God they've never inclined to going topless, thought Kit fervently. In the present circumstances that would have been unthinkable.

Carlos Santana squatted back on his heels to look at all three girls.

'Are you all, how do you say, ladies of leisure, or do you have an occupation?'

'No indeed,' Clem assured him. 'Katharine—only we call her Kit—is a pharmacist and we're both in art college.'

'Miss Katharine told us your home was in Wales?'

'Yes, near the town of Monmouth.' Clem glanced at Charity as she spoke, but Luis's proximity seemed to have rendered her twin uncharacteristically dumb. 'Do you both live here, Señor Santana?'

'Carlos, *por favor*,' he said earnestly. 'We are at the Hotel Florida.'

'We have friends staying there,' said Clem in surprise. 'They're usually down on the beach with us by this time, but we had a message this morning to say the boys aren't well—what we tourists call "Spanish tummy"!' She dimpled at Carlos in a way he obviously found quite irresistible, and Kit sighed inwardly. Things had been going too smoothly with the twins up to now. The advent of two attractive Spanish charmers was disturbing. Bruce and Angus McPherson were like two friendly boys next door. Los Señores Santana were something else entirely.

'I trust that none of you ladies has suffered any such ill effects?' enquired Luis gravely, his eyes unswerving on Charity's flushed face.

As her sister appeared incapable of speech Kit felt obliged to answer.

'Fortunately, no. Our father is a doctor, so as you can imagine we came away with a long list of instructions and various remedies just in case we succumbed in spite of his advice.'

'And as Kit herself is a pharmacist,' put in Clem, 'we daren't get ill or she will be affronted.'

There was general laughter, but Kit felt relegated to the role of elderly governess by Clem's ingenuous remark. Both men stood up, and Kit felt a little relieved at the prospect of their departure. Not for long, as she heard Carlos tender an invitation for lunch.

'That's extremely kind of you, but we're not dressed for it,' she said swiftly, ignoring the looks of disappointment turned on her by the twins.

'Then we could lunch here, if you will permit,' said Luis, waving an arm towards the beach restaurant.

'Oh yes, please,' said Chatty, suddenly finding her voice. 'We always lunch there anyway.'

In the face of this undeniable statement there was little Kit could do but accept gracefully, and she tied on her black and white pareu over its matching bikini with resignation. Her misgivings faded slightly as the five of them lunched together in great harmony, her sisters resisting the persuasion of the Santanas to try deep-fried calamares, amid much lighthearted banter. They joined Kit in their customary toasted sandwiches and lemonade, while the men ate squid and drank red wine, all of them finishing off with coffee. Initially Kit started out feeling like a spare wheel, but the faultless manners of the two men soon rid her of this and she was able to enjoy the protracted meal just as much as Charity and Clem. The former had found her tongue again and bubbled in her usual unaffected way, entertaining them all with stories of college life and some of the pranks she and Clem had perpetrated by masquerading as each other.

'It is easy to tell you apart when you are together——' Luis stopped as Carlos laughed at his phrasing. 'Cállete, Carlos. What I am trying patiently to say is that with your hair so, and wearing different clothes, I can tell which is Miss Clemency and which one is Miss Charity. But last night, in those identical white dresses——!'

'You noticed us last night?' asked Clem ingenuously.

'Señorita, there was not a man in the room who did not notice you!' Although Luis answered Clem, his look was patently for Charity, and her colour rose as his eyes held hers.

Both girls were wearing thin cotton shirts over their bikinis, and Chatty's scar was plainly visible as a small ridge of white on one golden thigh.

'They were born with no distinguishing marks at all——' began Kit,

'But I'm the awkward one,' interrupted Chatty, smiling. 'I fell on a broken bottle when I was little and I have this scar.'

Luis looked at it with an expression so like a caress on his face that Kit shifted uncomfortably in her seat, and Carlos Santana rose to his feet, obviously aware of her disquiet.

'We must leave you now, ladies,' he said, as Luis followed suit with obvious reluctance. 'However, will you allow us to make a suggestion? It would please us very much if you would care to take a short trip in a boat tomorrow and have lunch aboard; the picnic, I think you say.'

One look at the incandescent expressions on the twins' faces was enough to prevent Kit voicing the refusal that rose instinctively to her lips, and there was nothing she could do but accept gracefully.

'We shall be in the foyer of your apartment building at eleven in the morning, Miss Vaughan,' said Carlos, having learned their address, and after many flowery courtesies, both men departed, leaving the younger Vaughans to stare after them in excitement.

'Too many flies about to sit there with your mouths open,' said Kit tartly. 'Come on, back to the sunbathing.'

She spent quite a bit of time that afternoon handing out all sorts of sensible advice to unreceptive ears on the subject of holiday romances, plus the folly of getting involved with Spanish gentlemen, however young and charming they might be.

'But Luis—I mean *both* of them were very nice,' protested Chatty. 'And we promise not to be silly, don't we, Clem?'

'*I* won't,' said Clem cheerfully. 'Carlos was just as taken with Kit as me, but you were gazing at Luis like a constipated cow.'

'Don't be disgusting, I was not!' Charity turned on her fiercely. 'I was a little bit shy to begin with, that's all.'

'Which is a first, for a start.'

'Oh, shut up!'

Kit leaned across, waving an admonishing finger.

'That will do, my pretties, or I'll exert my in loco parentis bit and send a message to the delightful duo to the effect that Spanish tummy has overtaken you, too.'

'Kit, you wouldn't!'

'Try me.'

Vanquished, the twins lay peacefully in the lessening strength of the afternoon sun until it was time to leave and they wandered back to the flat.

'What shall we do now, Kit?' asked Clem. 'I know, could we tidy up a bit and go down to the shops at the marina?'

'There are plenty of shops up here,' said Kit, not fancying the prospect.

'We've seen all those. Please, Kit!'

'Oh, very well. I'll have a bath while you two ring from here to the Florida and enquire about Bruce and Angus.'

The twins had the grace to look guilty, and hurried off to the public telephone booths at the back of the foyer while Kit went up in the lift. She had a swift shower, emerging in time to let in Chatty and Clem.

'A bit better, but limp and very sorry for themselves, Mrs McPherson said,' reported Clem.

'Mr Mac has taken the girls to Mijas for the day and Mrs Mac is doing the Florence Nightingale bit. I offered some of our pills, but apparently they came well prepared,' said Chatty, 'so I explained about our boat trip and said we'd ring when we got back.'

'Well done! It wouldn't do to let Bruce and Angus feel neglected,' said Kit approvingly. 'Have your baths or showers now, and then we shan't have to bother later.'

Half an hour later they set off for the marina in the beautiful mellow light of sunset, enjoying the effect of the lamps just lighting up the palm-lined causeway and outlining the moorings of the marina.

'Beautiful,' sighed Clem blissfully. She turned impulsively to Kit. 'You were an angel to bring us, Kit. We are grateful.' She leaned across Kit to look meaningfully at Charity. 'I'll make sure she doesn't get too dimwitted about Don Juan, too.'

'Luis, not Juan,' said Chatty, unperturbed.

Kit laughed, refusing to let any anxiety spoil the evening. Charity and Clem had reverted to similar outfits again; short cotton jersey dresses in pale pink with batwing sleeves and a strip of bias-cut pink and white stripes let in at hip level in lieu of a belt. Kit's jeans were white, with a china-blue long-sleeved shirt knotted at the midriff. In the fading light their skins were copper tinted in the last rays of the sun.

'Well, at least we should all look very healthy when we get home,' remarked Kit. 'Here are the shops, as promised, and there's the boutique—Milagrita.'

'Wow—a bit pricey-looking!'

They all gazed at the contents of the shop window with attention, hoping to see something special for their mother. A grey kid belt caught Kit's eye and she pointed it out to the twins, who approved immediately.

'Matches Mother's new shoes—super!'

They went in, to be greeted by a girl about the same age as Kit, dressed in a sleeveless white dress of deceiving simplicity. She smiled in welcome, her grey eyes oddly familiar beneath light brown hair artfully streaked with ash blonde above an expertly made up face.

'Buenas tardes.' She hesitated, then changed to English. 'May I help you?'

Our nationality must be fairly obvious, thought Kit in amusement, and asked to see the belt they fancied. Several others were also produced for them to pore over and they spent a few minutes sifting through them before choosing the original grey one for Mrs Vaughan. While Kit was paying for it the other two were browsing through a rail of clothes marked down in price.

'It is the end of the season,' explained the Spanish girl. 'There is ten per cent off all the clothes in the store, but those on that rail are half-price.'

None of the girls could resist a bargain, and after checking their resources the twins decided they could manage a blouse each, and Kit was attracted to a pair of beautifully cut dark red trousers with a matching red skin belt. The twins shared one fitting room, chattering nineteen to the dozen, as usual, while Kit took the other cubicle at the other end of the elegant little shop. She stripped off her white jeans and was easing her way into the narrowly cut trousers when the shop door opened and, surprisingly, she heard a man's voice; what was more, she had heard it before, and recently. Very cautiously she peered through the curtains drawn across the cubicle and saw Reid Livesey lounging in the open doorway in his beachcomber outfit of ragged cut-offs and battered cap, though this time he had added an ancient white sweatshirt. Afraid to breathe, Kit shrank back against the wall, praying Charity and Clem would stay put. She frowned as she realised Reid had switched to English.

'Where's your brother and Luis this afternoon?' he was saying casually. Luis! There must be thousands in Spain—surely not the same one.

'Both of them have to be on duty at the hotel; the dining room and the bar are short-staffed,' answered the girl. 'They will both be fully occupied until at least midnight.'

'They managed a short break last night.'

'So I understand,' laughed the girl. 'Long enough to see two stunning girls!'

'As I know only too well.' The tone in Reid's voice made Kit cringe. 'They needled me into dancing with their older sister to get an introduction. I gather they were hoping to follow this up at the beach this morning to meet the nubile blondes.'

'Nubile? What is that?'

Kit's hackles rose at Reid's laugh, but the voices became indistinct as he and his companion moved through the doorway. Kit tore off the trousers and pulled on her jeans, leaving the cubicle to interrupt Charity and Clem who were putting on their own clothes.

'We're having these two white silk ones, Kit—what do you think?'

Kit gave a cursory glance at the garments and murmured something approving, relieved that the girls obviously hadn't heard Reid's remarks. She handed the trousers back to the girl in the white dress with a perfunctory apology, waiting with impatience while the twins paid for their purchases.

'Didn't the slacks fit, Kit?' asked Charity.

'No.' Kit set off up the causeway at a great pace, anxious to get away from the marina at top speed. The others followed, looking at each other with eyebrows raised.

'What's the matter, Kit?' Clem was breathless, trying to keep up. 'Did we take too long, or something; are you mad at us?'

'Not at you,' said Kit grimly. 'Let's go back and have a drink and I'll tell you all about it.'

When the three of them were sitting on the verandah of the apartment, long glasses of Campari and orange juice in front of them, she told them what she had overheard in the boutique.

'Your handsome Spaniards are probably waiters at the Florida,' finished Kit brutally, 'just the way we joked about at home.'

'Then what were they doing at the dance?' said Chatty mutinously.

'It was probably their time off; no doubt it's a great way to look out for any promising talent among the tourists.' Kit was deliberately merciless in her estimation of the Santanas, but the responsibility for her sisters weighed heavily on her shoulders.

'Funny the McPhersons didn't recognise them,' said Clem, frowning.

'No doubt a lot of Spaniards look similar when they're in the hotel uniform.'

Chatty sighed.

'They're not very typically Spanish-looking, though. Does this mean our boat trip is off, then, Kit?'

'I don't know,' said Kit frankly. 'I don't like to disappoint you, I admit, and at least I shall be there to keep an eye on things. It might be fun to catch out our Spanish Lotharios— I suppose they're hiring a boat to impress.'

'I don't really want to go under the circumstances,' said Chatty in a quiet little voice, then she sat up straight, finishing her drink. 'Though I can't really see what difference it makes. They haven't really tried to give us a line—what does it matter if they *are* waiters, and if that *is* Carlos's sister; well, lots of people work in shops. Are you being a bit snobbish, Kit?'

Kit was stung.

'Of course not! None of that matters. As long as you both have your eyes wide open you can enjoy your boat trip and that will be that.'

Clem had kept unusually silent.

'What's really burning you up is the fact that Reid Livesey apparently only danced with you because Luis and Carlos wanted an introduction.' Her eyes looked searchingly at Kit, who bit her lip and flushed.

'Yes, you're right. I'm hopping mad! I can't think how he's involved in all this. Never mind—let's forget about it for now and go down to the Italian restaurant for a pizza, or something. I don't feel like wandering far tonight.'

Despite the slight shadow cast over their outing, the twins were dressed and ready long before the appointed time next morning, after much discussion about what to wear, finally unable to resist putting on the new silk shirts. Otherwise they had completely different shorts and sneakers, Clem with her hair in a pigtail and Chatty with hers tied in bunches. They looked very young and sweet, contrasting with Kit's rather sophisticated outfit of long-sleeved black voile shirt knotted above white shorts, her hair tied back with a black and white striped scarf and large white hoops in her ears.

Obviously Luis Santana found the trio a delight to the eye, and was extravagant with his compliments when he arrived in the foyer with exact punctuality, though Kit had to suppress a rueful smile at Chatty's face when she saw his faded denims and obviously much-washed tee-shirt, which stretched across magnificent shoulders. Not over-tall, Luis had a splendid physique emphasised more by the shabby clothes he was wearing now than the elegant beach clothes of yesterday, or the immaculate suit worn at the dance. Chatty clearly felt he looked less aristocratic, supporting Kit's theory of false pretences, but the smile she gave him as he greeted her was very warm, nevertheless.

'You knew me, then,' she said. 'I covered up the scar purposely to test you.'

'I would know you in the dark,' he answered gravely, and there was a moment's silence before he collected himself to escort them down the esplanade and over to the marina, gleaming white like icing-sugar in the morning sun.

Kit remained quiet in the background while the twins talked away to Luis in their normal manner, telling him about buying their shirts at the boutique they could see over on the quay, the gilt of the name catching rays of light.

'Then you must have met my cousin,' said Luis, smiling. 'She was not too pleased at having to work again in the shop after a little holiday with Carlos and me. We all had to, how do you say, get down to it again yesterday.'

Kit was so interested in what Luis was saying, hoping for confirmation of her suspicions, that she only realised where he was leading them when he came to a halt beside a familiar-looking yacht.

'This is the *Golondrina*,' he said with a proud smile. 'Welcome aboard, *señoritas*.' He preceded them up the short gangplank at the stern of the boat and handed them up with a flourish, the twins' faces aglow with interest as they made their first acquaintance with a sea-going craft. Kit took Luis's hand reluctantly, wondering where Carlos was. A figure detached itself from the centre wheelhouse and her heart plummeted. It was not Carlos Santana.

'Good morning, Miss Vaughan.' The collected tones of the self-possessed voice could only belong to the ubiquitous Mr Livesey, and Kit had no option but to take the welcoming hand he held out.

'You know our friend Reid, of course,' said Luis. 'He will be coming with us, naturally.'

Naturally, echoed Kit silently, but she gave Reid a brilliant smile.

'An unexpected bonus,' she said sweetly.

The red-brown eyebrows flew up beneath the peak of the denim cap covering Reid's thick hair, his eyes dancing with pure enjoyment. Luis took the twins off to explore below decks, and Kit was left staring at her companion's bare brown torso with misgivings. The ragged denim cut-offs were all too familiar—a far cry from her urbane, if half-hearted, knight errant.

'Do I get the feeling you're just a little less than pleased to see me again, Miss Vaughan?' he enquired pleasantly, lounging against the glossy mahogany rail.

'Not at all,' she said carelessly. 'I just took a moment to resign myself to the inevitable. The quirks of fate and all that—it's certainly hellbent on throwing us together.'

'With what purpose, I wonder?' Reid was taking in her appearance with leisurely enjoyment, his smile widening at her patent displeasure.

'I thought Carlos was coming,' she said coolly.

'He is.' He stooped to pick up her holdall, and directed her towards the hatch just as the other three came up on deck.

'It's fabulous, Kit,' said Clem excitedly, 'so compact and gleaming, all that mahogany and brass looks so luxurious. I never imagined there would even be a sink and a gas cooker—*and* there's a loo and shower-compartment, and it sleeps six people!'

Chatty was silent for once, standing near Luis as he grinned at Clem's enthusiasm, her wide blue eyes on him searchingly now and again, as if trying to make up her mind what sort of man he was, but uncertain how to find out.

'Perhaps you would care to see for yourself,' suggested Reid indolently, 'and leave the younger element in the sunshine.'

Kit followed him below with something perilously near a flounce. She was only twenty-six, for God's sake, hardly geriatric quite yet! In spite of herself, she was equally impressed by the compact luxury of the yacht's fittings, and found the navy blue covers on the berths and navy and yellow curtains very much to her taste. Reid put her bag on one of the bunks and looked at her in enquiry.

'You approve?'

Kit found his half-clothed presence a little over-powering at such close quarters, and backed away slightly, ignoring the amusement in his irritatingly knowing eyes.

'Very attractive,' she admitted. 'Not in the least what I'd expected.'

'What do you find so surprising?'

'Your presence, for a start,' she said acidly. 'How do you happen to be here?'

'I am a friend of the Santanas; why not?' he answered carelessly, then went through to the galley to take some heavy tumblers from the small cupboard. 'From the noise above decks I imagine Carlos has arrived with the lunch, so take a few glasses with you, please. Let's join them for drinks.'

'Aye-aye, sir,' said Kit tartly, taking the tumblers from him with ill grace. The man was insufferable, filled with his own superiority, even looking like a ruffian in his present costume. She climbed up into the bright sunlight on deck, where Carlos had indeed arrived, together with a large picnic hamper and a refrigerated bag. A swarthy young man, dressed in conventional waiter's black and white, was just running down the gangplank to the quay.

'Hello, Carlos.' Kit smiled sweetly as he raised her hand for the customary almost-kiss on its back. 'One of your friends?'

The smiling grey eyes went blank for a moment.

'Julio? He helped carry the *almuerzo*—our lunch. How are you today, Señorita Catalina?'

Kit ignored her sisters, who were making faces at her behind his back while the other two saw to the drinks.

'Very well, Señor Santana. Thank you for inviting us to lunch on such a beautiful boat.'

His white teeth gleamed.

'Ketch, *señorita*—ketch. One must use the correct terms—nautical, is that right?'

'Yes indeed,' agreed Kit solemnly, accepting a glass of liquid that looked familiar. 'Let us by all means be accurate. This is Sangria, I presume. Thank you.'

The group settled down to a picnic lunch on the forward deck of the ketch.

'We could serve the meal in state below decks,' said Luis, 'but we thought you would prefer the sunshine.'

His guests agreed unanimously, though Kit insisted on sunhats as protection from the reflected noonday glare from the water. She had been provided with a small canvas seat near Reid, who stretched out on the deck beside her, gnawing on a chicken leg with no attempt at elegance while Kit sampled the delicious *empanadas* chosen from a varied selection of goodies in the hamper. The other four were talking incessantly, but Kit concentrated on enjoying her savoury fried pasty, making no attempt to join in, or to talk to the man beside her. He sat up and wiped his mouth on a napkin, foraging in the picnic basket for an orange, offering one to Kit. She took it, and dug her nails into the rind viciously to start peeling it.

'You have something against that orange?' Reid asked mildly, under cover of the buzz of noise from the others.

'No.'

'You looked remarkably belligerent when you attacked it—sublimating your passions?'

'Is psychology your hobby?' Kit removed her sunglasses to stare at him. Instantly he took off his own to look steadily back at her.

'It doesn't take a psychologist to see that you're labouring under the weight of that enormous chip on your shoulder, Katharine.'

'Kit,' she said automatically.

'I prefer Katharine—Kit is unisex. You are not.'

He leaned over and refilled her glass from the clinking jug of Sangria, and she drank some automatically, refusing to answer.

'What is it that's eating you? Aren't you enjoying your holiday?'

Kit was quiet for a moment, then she said with apparent inconsequence,

'I saw you yesterday.'

'I know.' He tilted the peak of his cap further over his eyes and settled himself more comfortably. Kit sat bolt upright, staring down at him.

'Where?'

'In the boutique.'

'But I wasn't—I mean I was——'

'You were in the cubicle trying something on. Of course I knew. Your sisters were talking non-stop in the other one; besides, the curtains don't quite reach the floor. I could see your feet. You have very expressive toenails.'

Kit had reached the age of twenty-six with very few digestive problems, but at the moment the feeling in her chest could only be described as what her grandmother called heartburn. *Empanadas*, oranges, Sangria, all combined with sheer rage, made an explosive combination. She took a deep breath, calming herself with an effort.

'What you said to the girl in the boutique——'

'Señora Carreras, you mean,' he said coldly.

A few more breaths did nothing to disperse the burning pain in Kit's chest and midriff.

'Señora Carreras,' she amended stiffly. 'Your conversation was solely for my benefit, then, as you began in Spanish and switched deliberately to English.'

He sat up straight and took off the disreputable cap.

'I confess to giving in to a sudden malicious impulse,' he said, looking very directly at her with a gaze that was chilling, despite the warmth of the sun. 'I admit freely that Luis and Carlos caught sight of your sisters at the dance the other night, and when I let slip that you were the beautiful tourist I'd driven back from Granada they gave me no peace until I asked you to dance and took you over to their table for an introduction.'

'Not your lucky day, was it!' said Kit bitterly.

'As things turned out, no,' he agreed. 'I took you back to your hosts as quickly as I could, hoping to explain before my two *amigos* put all four feet in it, but

when I stopped for a moment to do so you almost
started a fight. Public dressings down in front of a
roomful of people can hardly appeal to many men, and
I'm certainly not one of them. When fate delivered you
at Milagrita's just as I was coming towards the quay I
yielded to temptation. You require me to apologise?'

'I require nothing of you, Mr Livesey, thank you,'
said Kit with what she hoped was a faintly bored
expression on her face. She looked over at the other
four, who were laughing hilariously and obviously
having a fantastic time. Her eyes softened and she got
up with the idea of gathering the lunch things together.
Reid rose with her, but both Santanas shot to their feet
to intercept as they realised Kit's intention.

'No, no, Señorita Catalina, please sit down—we will
deal with all this; I can assure you we are experts.' Luis
waved her back to her seat while he and Carlos swiftly
gathered up the plates and leftovers.

Kit's eyes met those of the twins immediately, but
they just grinned at her.

'You are used to this sort of thing?' she asked
casually, aware that Reid was frowning down at her,
eyes narrowed.

'Oh yes,' said Carlos blithely. 'My father makes very
sure of that.'

Kit's feelings were mixed, but she kept silent as the
hamper was taken below and Reid checked on the
engine. The three girls went below to tidy themselves
before the next part of the outing, and the twins were so
bubbling over with the wonderful time they were having
that Kit had no heart to damp down their high spirits.
When they went up on deck the three men were
chatting in the bows, and the two young Spaniards
smiled a welcome.

'I shall commandeer Katharine aft as navigator,' said
Reid, to Kit's surprise, 'while you children have fun
forard.'

Kit found herself meekly following Reid through to
the cockpit to stand beside him as he started the engine
and took the wheel while Carlos and Luis cast off. The
graceful *Golondrina* slowly edged away from the marina

and set off at a steady pace for the open sea. Despite herself Kit felt a thrill of exultation.

'Do you really want me to navigate?'

'Not in the least,' said Reid bluntly. 'I'm giving the youngsters a break without your long face to sour the proceedings.'

She was speechless for a moment, staring at the tall, muscular figure as he handled the craft with such effortless competence.

'You have a nerve——' she began, but he turned such a hostile eye on her that she was instantly quelled.

'I don't know what you have against Carlos and Luis,' he said coldly, 'but you certainly have a strange attitude towards them. They're good lads, perfectly trustworthy, yet you behave as though they'd just robbed a bank.'

Kit swallowed hard, partly to try to rid herself of the lump that seemed permanently lodged in her chest, and partly to calm herself down. She stared across the swept-back coachroof towards the bows, where the girls were hanging on to the rail, excitement and pleasure in every line of their bodies, their faces glowing and animated as their companions pointed out various landmarks along the coast while the ketch, her sails furled, glided over the blue water. How could she explain to the wretched man how protective she felt about Charity and Clem? The responsibility for their welfare sat firmly on her own shoulders during this brief holiday in a foreign country, and no harm of any sort, mental or physical, should come to them if she could possibly prevent it, both from her own point of view, and her promise to her parents.

The two Santanas were obviously much more exciting company than the young McPhersons, both in age and looks, but Kit was filled with doubt about them. If they *were* waiters it didn't matter in the least, only the fact that they were deliberately misleading the twins with this false show of luxury. And where did Reid Livesey fit into all this? He was a lot older than the Santanas, early thirties at a guess, and gave out an unmistakable aura of, if not wealth, at least a secure background. There was a simple solution, of course. She merely had to ask Reid about Carlos and Luis, she knew very well, but the thought of doing so intensified her indigestion to an unbearable degree. Suddenly she remembered the silver Mercedes, and her brows knotted.

'Couldn't you at least try to *look* as though you're enjoying yourself?' her companion said, his voice harsh above the muted rumble of the diesel engine.

Kit glared at him, stung.

'I was thinking,' she snapped.

'Nothing very pleasant, by the frown on your face—you'll get wrinkles.'

'I merely have a little indigestion,' she said with dignity.

'For someone who looks such a honey-pot you certainly are a bundle of ailments,' he said unforgivably. 'You'll find Alka-Seltzer in the hanging locker in the galley; try some.'

Kit obeyed with a speed prompted mainly by a desire for privacy to mop up the tears that suddenly welled up behind the dark lenses. She yanked open the hanging locker viciously, found the Alka-Seltzer and stood sipping the fizzing liquid until the tumult inside her quietened a little. 'Bundle of ailments', indeed! Until the stupid labyrinthitis she had hardly known a day's illness in her life. Well, she had been against coming on this holiday from the start, and her forebodings were proving right. If ever she were fool enough to marry and have children she would pray for boys and let someone else worry about their daughters! Kit replaced the Seltzer, washed and dried the glass she'd used, put it away and marched out to rejoin Reid Livesey, who was turning the ketch in a wide, graceful arc out to sea.

'What's over there?' she asked, determined to be polite and pleasant if it killed her—which, considering how painful it was to accomplish, seemed a distinct possibility.

'Tangier. But we won't venture that far.'

Kit smiled brightly and waved at Charity and Clem, who had noticed her absence and were obviously reassured at the impression of enjoyment she was doing her utmost to put across. It could have been a lovely day if only—she stopped her train of thought instantly as Reid said unexpectedly,

'Like a turn at the wheel?'

She gave a startled nod and slid in front of him, putting her hands on the wheel where his had been.

'You can drive a car?' His breath was warm on her neck, and she nodded dumbly, hardly daring to move.

'Go on then—steer. I'm right here behind you, don't worry.'

But that's precisely what *is* worrying me, she thought, and tossed her head impatiently. Reid moved even closer, obviously thinking she was nervous.

'All right?'

'Fine!'

The others in the bow suddenly realised they had a new helmsman and waved madly, the Santanas clasping their hands above their heads and shouting something Kit couldn't hear, but was obviously in congratulation. Greatly daring, she turned the wheel a little, veering slightly to the left towards the coast, then setting a straight course again, taking a deep breath of satisfaction that brought her shoulders squarely back against Reid's hard, bare chest. Instantly she moved as far forward as possible, which was very little and a complete waste of time, as he promptly moved up close behind her again, leaving no further room for manoeuvre.

'Checkmate,' he said softly, barely audible above the engine, but too close to her ear to miss his meaning.

'I don't play chess,' she said coolly, concentrating on the course ahead.

'I could teach you,' he offered, sliding his arms round her waist and drawing her the last fraction against him, so that they were in close contact from shoulder to knee.

'You don't play fair. I'm not in the best of positions to remove your hands, Mr Livesey,' she said repressively.

'I know. I've never thought of this before,' he said,

with hypocritical surprise. 'If you take your hands off the wheel who knows what will happen to the *Golondrina*; we could end up on the coast of Morocco!'

Kit stood motionless, feet riveted to the deck, afraid to release the wheel, even more apprehensive about the long-fingered hands that not only held her so firmly against him, but were beginning to rove, one reaching upward, the other spreading over her stomach, pressing her so tightly against him that certain unmistakable physical reactions in his body were impossible to ignore.

'Mr Livesey——' she gasped.

'Reid,' he said into her neck.

'Please——'

'Say Reid.' His lips rested against her hot skin and his tongue slid to caress the hollow behind her ear. Panic filled her. The other four in the front were completely oblivious to anything going on in the stern. They were too far out from the shore to be visible to anyone else, and for a few hot, drumming moments Kit was frantic.

'Reid!' she almost sobbed.

Immediately his hands withdrew, he stepped back a little, and Kit slid from behind the wheel, heedless of whether he was ready to take over or not. Apparently he was, as nothing untoward happened to the ketch, and without looking at the unperturbed figure at the wheel she fled below and sponged her face in the galley to cool down cheeks that glowed like infra-red lamps. Next holiday I'll go to the Shetlands, or Outer Mongolia, she thought fiercely. Heaven protect me from amatory holiday Romeos! It wasn't Carlos and Luis she should have been worrying about—it was Mr Lordly Livesey who was the wolf in wolf's clothing. Thank the lord Charity and Clem were too young for *him*, anyway. Kit assured herself that she could look after herself, but her knees were knocking like a flamenco dancer's castanets, and it was quite a while before she felt sufficiently recovered to join what Reid had so pointedly called the younger element in the bows.

The twins turned ecstatic, happy faces to her as she moved in beside them.

'Isn't this great?' they said in complete unison.

Carlos and Luis laughed delightedly as Kit assured them the twins always spoke as one girl when excited.

'They are so fascinating,' declared Luis ingenuously, and something suddenly occurred to Kit.

'You both speak extraordinarily good English,' she commented.

'They went to business college in the U.K.,' said Chatty, beaming. 'They've even been to Cardiff!'

'A beautiful city,' said Carlos, 'ah, Reid is taking us in; there is the marina ahead, and over to the left you can see the Hotel Florida, and the Apartamientos Teresa. Did you enjoy helming the *Golondrina*?'

'Very much,' Kit smiled, keeping her reservations about the experience to herself.

To her surprise it was after five by the time the ketch was secured at her mooring once more.

'I hope you won't be late,' said Kit anxiously, as she thanked both young men. They looked blank.

'It is not late,' said Luis, 'in fact I am desolated that we must part so early.'

The look in Chatty's eyes plainly agreed with this statement, but she appeared to be suffering another of the unusual attacks of dumbness affecting her lately, and it was left to Clem to give rapturous thanks for their heavenly day. Reid stood silent throughout the interchange, his face wearing its usual bland mask. His peaked cap was discarded and he had put on an ancient white sweater which, if anything, was even less distinguished than his shorts. He put out a hand to touch the sleeve of Clem's new white silk shirt.

'You've picked up a smear of oil,' he pointed out.

Clem gave a squeal of dismay, then did her best to look unaffected.

'My own fault for wearing a new shirt—we wanted to show off our new purchases,' she said ruefully.

'Where did you buy it?' asked Carlos.

'Over there on the quay at that super boutique. Never mind, I'm sure it will wash.'

'Do not disturb yourself, I shall replace it. Milagrita will have another, I'm sure.'

'Oh no!' Kit was horrified. 'Please, it will be no trouble to wash, I assure you; they were silly to wear silk on a boat. Besides, it was very expensive.'

Carlos seemed to retreat, and with great dignity he said,

'As you wish.'

Now what have I said? thought Kit in desperation. Finally she turned to Reid, to find him watching her like a cat who has just learnt how to open the birdcage.

'Thank you for letting me take the helm for a while,' she said unwillingly.

'Don't thank me, thank them.' Her jerked his head towards Carlos and Luis. 'It's their boat, not mine.'

For a moment Kit felt as blank as the look on the Santanas' faces. She looked at them, avoiding her sisters' eyes, then turned back to Reid.

'But I thought you. . . .' her voice died away at the irony in his eyes.

'You thought I owned the *Golondrina*?' He shook his head before going on in an irritatingly confidential tone, 'You also thought Carlos and Luis here had borrowed or even hired the ketch to make a false impression on the beautiful Vaughan sisters, am I right?' He laughed, making Kit's skin crawl, and turned to the two unsmiling young men. 'I have an idea Miss Katharine here thinks you two are a couple of beach boys on the make, *amigos*!'

CHAPTER FIVE

THE three girls walked back to the apartment in complete silence. Kit felt shattered. The only coherent thought her mental processes seemed capable of producing was deep, bitter regret about her mother's broken ankle, and for all the wrong reasons. If Mrs Vaughan had been with them perhaps this militant urge to guard the twins would never have materialised. After all, they were in college the rest of the year, away from parental authority, and left to conduct themselves with the sense and innate good behaviour learned from Angharad Vaughan's skilful upbringing. How skilful her mother actually was had been brought home very clearly to Kit over these past few days. Without ever appearing to exert undue authority both parents managed to lay down fairly clear guide lines of behaviour. Kit realised that her own temporary guardianship of Charity and Clem had lacked balance; heavy on care and light on trust.

Neither girl said one word to her as they went up in the lift and Kit unlocked the door of the flat in an atmosphere of unrelieved gloom.

'We'd better pop back downstairs,' said Clem quietly to Chatty, then turned instantly to Kit. 'Just to ring up the McPhersons and ask how they are.'

Kit winced at Clem's automatic move to explain herself.

'Sure,' she said wearily. 'I'm for a bath. Take the key with you and have a look round the shops if you like.'

'In that case we'll have a quick wash and change our clothes,' said Chatty unexpectedly. 'You can't go out in a dirty blouse, Clem.'

They were extremely quick. No doubt at the thought of an hour's respite from my company, thought Kit, as she looked through an ancient copy of *Harpers Bazaar*, feeling like the wicked witch of the North. The twins emerged from their bedroom in jeans and sweatshirts.

72

'It's getting a little chilly,' said Clem, as they said goodbye.

It certainly seemed that way, thought Kit wearily, as she collected her tale of passion and peril. The warm bath did a great deal to relax her, but, buoyant as the water was, it did nothing to lift her spirits. The girls had nobly offered no word of censure after Kit's gaffe down on the marina—she wished they had; it would have been more bearable than their silent forbearance. After Reid's regrettably gloating little words of enlightenment her mistake and previous suspicions had all been suddenly revealed to the Spaniards, that was painfully obvious. Two friendly young men had been instantly transformed into remote, grave *hidalgos* who made their adieux with extreme formality, watched with sardonic pleasure by Reid Livesey, an ironic expression in eyes that gleamed ferally in the sunset light.

What one might term the end of a perfect day, concluded Kit, deciding there was no point in wallowing in misery. She had been the one to spoil things for Charity and Clem, so now she would just have to try to do her best to do whatever they wanted for the rest of their time—all five days of it. The evening stretched ahead with all the attraction of a wet bank holiday. At least her indigestion seemed to have gone, which was fairly amazing in the circumstances. Wearily she got out of the bath and dried herself, then put on her dressing-gown and lay on the bed watching the light drain from the sky to be replaced by reflections from the neon signs of some of the nearby hotels. The rumble of the traffic from the street below came up as a constant background, and almost lulled by the incessant muted accompaniment she slid into a light doze.

She was rudely awakened by an ungentle hand shaking her and Chatty bawling in her ear.

'Wake up, Kit—come on, wake up!'

She sat up with care, her eyes blinking in the glare of the overhead light, and quickly turned on her bedside lamp, motioning Chatty to switch the other one off, pearing at her watch.

'Lord, it's after eight—have you just come in?'

'Of course not, we've changed our clothes as well—
we thought you would wake of your own accord, but I
had to give you a shake finally. Hurry up and get
dressed, Kit, we're about to have visitors.'

'What!'

'Yes—put some clothes on, *please!*'

Kit looked in surprise as Clem threw some clean
underwear at her and rummaged in the wardrobe.

'What do you want to wear?' her sister demanded.

'I don't care.' Kit did up her bra and accepted an ink-
blue full-sleeved voile shirtwaister, putting it on with
speed. 'Who's visiting us, for heaven's sake?'

Both girls suddenly stood together, arms round each
other. Kit recognised the stance; it was their back-to-
the-wall, twins-against-the-world attitude. It must be
the thirteenth, or something, she thought wildly.

'Speak, for heaven's sake!'

'Carlos and Luis would like a word,' they said in a
rush.

'Here? Now?' Kit brushed her hair energetically, abandoning it to hang loose. She turned on the girls,
realising that tonight the double act was back in full
force, down to the last detail, navy and white sailor
dresses, low-heeled white pumps with demure bows,
hair clipped behind their ears with pearl slides.
'Why?'

'They want to talk to you for a moment,' said Clem,
as Chatty seemed tongue-tied. 'They should be here in
five minutes.'

'Give them a drink when they arrive, then—as long
as they like Campari; or we could open the dry sherry
we bought for Dad. Offer it anyway.'

A libation to the gods, Kit thought frantically, as she
made up her eyes with a touch of the same smoky shade
as her dress, and threaded silver hoops through her
earlobes. She pushed her feet into pale grey sandals,
sprayed herself with Carven's 'Madame' and she was
ready to walk out into the little lounge looking a great
deal more assured than she felt. Two faultlessly dressed
young men sprang to their feet, in expensively tailored
suits, hand-made shoes, shirts and ties impeccable, both

of them obviously dressed as elegantly as possible for the occasion.

'*Buenas noches*, Señorita Vaughan.'

After the ceremonial hand-kissing Kit invited them to sit down with a pang, sadly aware she was no longer 'Señorita Catalina'.

'We have come to apologise,' began Luis. Kit sat erect with surprise.

'*You* are apologising?' She felt baffled.

Clem, who was perched side by side with Charity on the high stools at the tiny bar, looked anxiously at Kit.

'When we went back out we did ring the McPhersons, as we said——'

'How are they?' asked Kit automatically.

'The girls have gone down with it now, but Bruce and Angus should be around again by tomorrow.' Clem glanced at Charity, who took up the story.

'We didn't go shopping. I asked Clem to go back to the marina with me and see if Luis—and Carlos—were still there.' She smiled uncertainly at Kit, who motioned her to go on. 'They were still at the boat with Reid, so we explained how you had the idea they'd just hired the boat, and were trying to con us.'

Kit shot an apprehensive look at the two young men sat opposite her, but was relieved to see a faint smile on both attractive faces.

Luis leaned forward earnestly, his hands clasped between his knees.

'We were both offended at first, *es verdad*, but when Charity explained how they could not have come without you; that your mother had an accident which prevented her from accompanying you, and that you feel responsible for *las hermanitas*——' he flashed a warm smile at the anxious faces of the twins, 'we understand very well how you felt.'

'I had no wish to offend you,' said Kit quietly. 'I am several years older than Clem and Charity——'

'*No lo creo*,' grinned Carlos. 'You do not expect us to believe that!'

'Thank you,' said Kit with dignity. 'I wasn't fishing for compliments, merely explaining that it is quite a responsibility to have care of two girls as pretty as Charity and Clem. They attract attention everywhere they go. I trust you will forgive my naturally suspicious nature, gentlemen.'

'*Por supuesto*, Señorita Catalina.' Carlos jumped to his feet to take Kit's hand to his lips again. 'Your mind may be easy; no harm shall come to your sisters, we assure you. Now, explanations are over. Permit us to invite you to dinner.'

The imploring look on both her sisters' faces silenced the instinctive refusal on Kit's lips. She stood up as they jumped down from their stools.

'You are very kind; such hospitality is overwhelming—lunch yesterday and the picnic today . . .'

'The hotel prepared that, it was no trouble.' Luis brushed her doubts aside, smiling at Chatty in a way that made her eyes glow.

'How long are you staying at the Florida?' Kit locked the verandah doors and turned to see a rather odd look on the faces of both young men.

'I live there,' said Carlos, 'and temporarily so does Luis. My father owns it and we help him. Normally I manage the Florida here, and Luis manages Padre's other hotel in Marbella, but at the moment we are on holiday, just like you, except for emergencies.'

Kit just sat, shattered. After a while she glanced up at the twins.

'Did *you* know all this?'

They denied this vehemently.

'At least,' amended Charity, with a smile at Luis, 'not until this evening. I can't say I was all that curious about occupation and status, and all that.'

This rather pointed little statement did nothing to raise Kit's spirits.

'Why don't the four of you go out together tonight?' she said, trying to sound cheerful. 'You don't need me along this evening. I'll make myself something here.'

There were adamant refusals from both the Santanas and Charity and Clem.

'It would be more fitting if you were present, Señorita Kit,' said Luis with such finality she gave in.

'But only if you drop the "Miss" and call me Kit,' she said with a smile. 'And please could we go somewhere other than your hotel!'

Wherever she desired, she was assured, and eventually an Indonesian restaurant was the final choice, which reassured her no end. The possibility of stumbling over Reid Livesey there seemed reasonably remote, and she set out for her evening in a much happier frame of mind than had seemed possible earlier on.

Both young Spaniards courteously made every effort to ensure that Kit felt at ease during the evening, with no hint of being the odd one out. Luis, it was true, tended to become absorbed exclusively in Charity every now and then, but his cousin was scrupulously attentive to both Kit and Clem, and what was more, provided a few interesting details about the enigmatic Mr Livesey while they enjoyed the Nasi Goreng and various other unfamiliar Indonesian dishes presented to them in abundance.

Carlos had apparently met Reid at the Boat Show in London at Earls Court early in the year, and spent several evenings with him during his stay in London.

'He works in a bank,' he said casually, 'and I visited his flat several times. He gave me much helpful advice when I buy—bought—the *Golondrina*.'

'Did you meet his wife?' put in Clem, her face the picture of innocence.

'He does not have one. He is a, how do you say, a bachelor.' Carlos smiled at her indulgently. 'Why? You like him?'

'Naturally—very *macho*!' Clem licked her fingers, avoiding Kit's glacial eye with great care. 'Does he come to Spain much?'

'Quite often. I believe he has to travel a great deal in his work.'

In banking? Kit was thoughtful as she refused further offers of food, accepting strong black coffee in place of dessert.

'He has stayed at the Florida for two weekends during the summer,' said Luis. 'He combines business with the love of his life—sailing.'

'In fact,' added Carlos, 'he was kind enough to accompany us back to Marina Costa from Poole in England for the ketch's first trip. You have a name for it, *no*?'

'Maiden voyage?' said Kit.

'Ah, *sí*. I took my sister, and *mi primo* here, to England to meet Reid in Dorset, and we all came back in the *Golondrina*. It was very pleasant, but next week we must get back to work. It is quieter now, of course, but we take many winter bookings at the Florida, and there is always work to be done.'

Something was niggling at Kit.

'Does your sister prefer to work in the boutique rather than in the hotel?' she asked curiously.

'Oh yes,' said Carlos carelessly. 'She prefers to be independent. Besides, it is an absorbing interest since her husband died. Milagrita has been a widow for three years.'

Kit looked at Carlos with resignation.

'And she owns the shop, of course.'

'But of course. Reid did not tell you?'

She shook her head, lips tightening. Reid had told her nothing at all, obviously taking delight in watching her put her foot in it at every turn all day. She uttered a silent, secret prayer for just one, solitary opportunity to discomfit Reid in any way possible, coming back to earth to hear Carlos telling Clem that Reid and Milagrita had gone to Marbella for the evening in his sister's Mercedes. I hope he gets food poisoning thought Kit childishly.

The evening ended with arrangements for another picnic lunch aboard the ketch next day, despite Kit's protests that the hospitality was all one-sided. She was assured that it was a negligible return for the pleasure and honour of the ladies' company. On the way back to the apartment the twins told their hosts about the McPherson boys and their misfortune. To their everlasting credit, as far as Kit was concerned, both Santanas offered to include the Scots boys on the boat trip if they felt well enough next day, promising to send an invitation to their room first thing in the morning. The luminous smile Charity turned on Luis almost stopped him in his tracks, and Kit found it in her heart to be sorry for the young Spaniard, who would obviously have liked some moments alone with her sister. It was equally obvious that he expected no such favour to be granted, and there was a general leavetaking, with reiterated thanks from the three sisters as they entered the lift.

Due to her prolonged sleep earlier in the evening Kit was awake for some time after she went to bed. It had been quite a day, one way and another, revelations coming thick and fast. As far as the twins were concerned she now felt they could look after themselves. The Santana cousins had gone out of their way to emphasise their intentions, and one fact was beginning to emerge with clarity. The prospect of another day anywhere near Reid Livesey was beginning to give her indigestion again. She got up irritably to find the phial of Alka-Seltzer in her case, after which she read herself into a state of somnolence, putting thoughts of Reid firmly from her mind.

Over breakfast next morning Kit announced to the twins that she would much rather spend the day quietly on the beach than idle around the Mediterranean on the Santanas' ketch.

'But Kit,' began Chatty, 'we don't like to think of you alone while we're off enjoying ourselves.'

'Idiot child—sometimes being alone and peaceful is the way I enjoy myself most. I'm a separate entity, not half of a whole like you two.' Kit poured out coffee and looked out to sea from the verandah with her usual pleasure in the sunlit view. 'I found an old Georgette Heyer I haven't read, I have my suntan oil and absolutely no qualms about lunching alone at the beach restaurant. Besides, we older women need a little rest now and then.'

Clem looked at her doubtfully.

'If you're sure you'll be all right. We said we'd stop by the Florida at ten, collect the McPhersons if they're coming, and meet Carlos and Luis down at the boat.'

'Great!' Kit was emphatic. 'You do that. Take a key and I'll expect you when I see you.'

'We keep forgetting that you're still convalescent,' said Chatty remorsefully. 'You look so marvellous with a tan it's hard to remember you were all wobbly and sickly only a short time ago. You really do feel all right?'

'Really!' said Kit firmly. 'Now do me a favour and wash these cups and plates, which will ease your unnecessary consciences, whereupon I shall get my things together and go down to the beach early. I have a specific spot in mind, so I'd better get on my bike.'

The three girls left the apartment together, parting at the path that ran down to the terrace above the beach. This was virtually deserted at this time of day, only the wooden bases out in rows, waiting for the gaily-coloured mattresses to cover their skeletons. The man in charge of them hastened to lay out two mattresses where Kit indicated, and she paid for the use of both of them, dumping her large white bag on one. She stripped off her pareu and lay down on the other with a sigh, reaching for her novel. After the flamboyant Esmeralda it was a relief to follow the more cerebral adventures of one of Miss Heyer's more prosaic heroines, who seemed to cope with the sarcastic, domineering hero with a facility Kit greatly envied. It was peaceful in the bright, newly-washed light of early morning. For the time being the sleepy-looking waiters at the restaurant stood gossiping and yawning in a group, without the need for music so early in the day. The pedal boats stood idle, and the sand was untrammelled by junior construction outfits for the time being, Kit's only companions the silent fishermen sitting motionless beside their lines on the jetty.

With a sigh of contentment she plunged back into the world of Regency London and became absorbed in her book, hardly aware of the passage of time until the first notes of a Spanish love song came through the amplifiers, and the sound of multilingual conversation all round her told her the Costa del Sol had woken up. Casting a glance around her, she could see no sign of the McPhersons, and went on with her novel in pure contentment. Her little bubble of peace and tranquillity was rudely shattered some time later when her white holdall hit the sand with a thump and two long, tanned legs came into her line of vision on the mattress next to hers. With superhuman effort Kit kept her eyes glued on the page she was reading.

'Aren't you going to say good morning?' enquired a familiar voice pleasantly, and she slowly put down her book, turning to look at Reid Livesey without welcome, all her pleasure in her peaceful solitude completely dispelled. He smiled guilelessly, his eyes alight with unholy mirth under the shade of the canopy.

'Good morning,' she said flatly, then returned to her book.

'Are you going to ask me why I'm here?'

Kit looked at his dark face dispassionately.

'No. It's a public beach. Any objections I might have are no doubt useless, apart from which I feel sure you're about to enlighten me anyway.'

'Completely accurate. What a clinical lady you are on occasion!' Hands clasped behind his head, he examined her from her painted toenails to the thick plait of glossy dark hair. 'I find it hard to equate the poised perfection of today with the clinging damsel in Granada trying to communicate in fractured Spanish.'

'All part of the female instinct to keep the male guessing.' Kit refused to rise.

'So it's the cool mystery bit this morning.' Reid turned his dark red head so that she had no possibility of escaping the almost tangible quality of his look.

'To be accurate, I was merely aiming for peace and privacy.' She gave him a pointed little smile and returned to the printed page, which might have been printed with hieroglyphics rather than English prose, for all the sense it made. There was no use in losing her temper. She clung to her calm like a drowning man to a spar, and tried to analyse just precisely what this man possessed to make her lose her cool so quickly. She paid attention to what he was saying with an effort.

'When the twins turned up with the young Scots boys I felt redundant,' he said amicably. 'They told me where you were, so I thought you might be glad of company.'

'Ecstatic!'

'Now don't be sarcastic.' Reid looked at her in mock reproof, then suddenly grinned at her with the first really friendly expression on his face since her first fleeting glimpse of him on the deck of the ketch. 'Shall we call a truce, if only for today, Miss Katharine Vaughan?'

Kit looked at him thoughtfully.

'I don't know why, after all the hot water you took delight in landing me in with such relish. Why?'

He appeared to think it over for a while before saying slowly,

'It's quite difficult to know why. I think it's your habit of thinking the worst of people; the human race seems to be guilty until proved innocent as far as you're concerned.'

Kit swallowed the acid retort that rose to her lips, and waited in silence for him to continue.

'After all,' he went on, 'it was you who kept on about not 'presuming on our meeting' or some such rubbish, if we happened to meet again. Not my idea, you'll admit. Then you jumped to the worst possible conclusions about Carlos and Luis, which got me on the raw a little. Would it have been so awful if they *had* been waiters, or shop assistants, instead of part of a wealthy family?'

'I seem to have been explaining myself to someone for the past two days,' said Kit wearily. 'My objection was that they were passing themselves off as something they were not to make the running with Charity and Clem. As it happens I was wrong. I've apologised to them both. I see no need to apologise to you, Reid, as you were the one who deliberately tried to mislead me. Now shall we drop the subject?'

Without waiting for an answer she turned back to her book and with dogged determination forced her attention back to the story.

'As I said before, Katharine,' Reid's voice was deep and persuasive, penetrating Kit's defences despite all her resolution, 'shall we call a truce for today—or even better, a cease-fire?'

'Very well,' she said, in a laudably matter-of-fact manner. 'I'll do my best not to fire the first hostile salvo. Have you brought a book?'

Reid nodded his head, pointing to *Schindler's Ark* on the towel beside him. He had discarded his disreputable cut-offs and was the epitome of the elegant resort habitué, in brief black swimming trunks, with a thin lawn shirt in black and white dogtooth checks hanging in casual intimacy from the nail where her pareu fluttered in the breeze.

At first Kit found it difficult to concentrate on her novel, but after a while, when it became obvious that her companion was thoroughly absorbed in his own book, the story recaptured her full attention and she raised her eyes vaguely when her companion roused her with a quiet,

'Katharine!'

'M-m?'

'It's well after midday. Shall we take advantage of our early start and have lunch while it's still quiet?' Reid stood looking down at her and held out his hand. She took it and got quickly to her feet, accepting her pareu sleepily, tying it round her with a firm yank of the ends. She spread her towel on her mattress, took her purse from the large bag, then left the latter underneath the sunbed.

'Why do you want your purse?' Reid was shrugging into his shirt as they made their way over the warm sand. He stepped up on the restaurant's raised platform, holding out a hand to help her up after him, and led her over to a table in the shade. Kit looked at him steadily across the checked paper tablecloth and sighed.

'I'm beginning to feel like a parasite. For the past few days I just don't seem to be paying my way at all.'

The arrival of the waiter halted her, and, after some persuasion from Reid, she agreed to crayfish and salad, instead of her usual sandwich, listening to him ordering fluently, with an accent that sounded highly authentic.

'So tell me why you're a parasite,' said Reid, settling back in his chair.

Kit's heavy-lidded eyes dropped to her fingers, which were pleating the paper napkin.

'We've had dinner with the McPhersons, with Carlos and Luis last night, lunch on the boat, lunch here the day before that. No one will let us pay for anything in return.'

'From this am I to gather you wish to pay for my lunch?'

Kit stole a look at him under her lashes, reassured to see him grinning.

'Well, it would be . . .'

Reid shook his head decisively.

'No way! You can be as liberated as you like elsewhere, but if a female forked out to a Spanish waiter for any meal I ever ate I rather fancy my id would never recover.'

'What nonsense!' Kit laughed with genuine amusement, her eyes lighting up as they gleamed mock-censure. 'You men and your machismo!'

'We have to hang on to something.' He spread his hands in mock deprecation. 'Your sex is eroding our male prerogatives with relentless persistence; allow us what little privileges we can still claim!' He smiled at her in approval. 'You should do that more often, you know.'

'Do what?'

'Laugh. I've never seen you laugh properly before.'

Kit leaned her elbows on the table, her chin in her hands, looking back at him without constraint.

'Since I met you, Mr Livesey, I seem to have lost the knack, for some reason. You really were rather malevolent about all the wrong impressions I was tangled up in. A couple of informed little words here and there would have set me straight in a matter of seconds. Instead of which you took infinite pleasure in watching me flounder.'

'Perhaps I should point out that your little misconceptions were by no means the only pleasure I enjoyed to the full yesterday.' He lounged easily in his chair, completely relaxed, but the hazel-yellow eyes held a warmth Kit found disconcerting. She looked away and sat upright.

'Yes. I could hardly fail to notice.'

The waiter arrived at that moment with a bottle of chilled white wine and a basket of crusty rolls, returning almost immediately with the crayfish and an enormous platter of mixed salad which he set down in the middle of the table with a flourish. Kit looked at it in amused awe.

'That's enough for four!'

'Nonsense. You don't eat enough for a growing girl, if yesterday's lunch was anything to go by.' He spooned a large helping of salad on her plate and filled their glasses. 'Now. While we eat you can fill me in on the normal background and occupation of Miss Katharine Vaughan. Do you have another name?'

'Angharad—after my mother.'

'Very pretty, but a little difficult to the untutored tongue!' Reid raised his glass in salute.

Kit tasted a little of the wine, enjoying the delicious chilled tang after her morning in the sun.

'Your tongue sounds anything but untutored to me,' she said.

'I was asking about you. Then if you have sufficient interest I'll return the compliment. Eat some bread.'

Kit did as he ordered, starting on her potted life history with mouth full.

'Katharine Angharad Vaughan, age twenty-six, hardly to be considered as still a growing girl at time of going to press.' She dimpled at him. 'Born in Llanhowell, in the vicinity of Monmouth, where she was educated, until college in Bath to train as pharmacist and, eventually, to work in father's medical practice. Eldest of family of four, enjoys tennis, dancing, theatre, music, reading, etc., etc.' She ate a mouthful of succulent fish with enjoyment. 'M'm, lovely. Now your turn.'

Reid leaned towards her.

'Haven't you left out a fairly important part?'

'I don't think so.'

'How about men; attachments?'

'How about them? A fair amount—normal for the average female, but nothing very deep and meaningful,

I'm afraid.' Kit smiled cheekily at Reid. 'Come on; fair's fair. I know you work in a bank, according to Carlos, and I know you're heavily into sailing, also that you speak Spanish, or Castilian or whatever.'

'Portignol, to be precise.' Reid grinned at her puzzled look and refilled her glass. 'I was born and brought up in Brazil, and because my second language from birth is Portuguese I speak a sort of mixture of Portuguese and Spanish that gets me by very well in Spanish-speaking countries.'

Kit put down her fork, frowning at him.

'Is it true that you work in a bank, then?'

'Yes. I've been, to use a rather picturesque English phrase, in merchant banking in London for the past three years. I'm thirty-four, my parents are Anglo-Brazilian; i.e. English ancestry, fourth generation to be born in Brazil. They own a *fazenda*, a large farm or ranch, the main part of whose output is tobacco. They also run sheep and cattle. The *fazenda* is in the state of Rio Grande do Sul, near Porto Alegre—near by Brazilian standards, that is.' He paused. 'Am I boring you?'

Kit's deceptively sleepy eyes flew open and she shook her head vigorously.

'I'm riveted. Please go on.'

'My father does less these days; my brother virtually runs the place. He's my senior by a year.'

'What's his name?'

'Richard, baptismally. But when he was small the local children used to taunt him with shouts of "*Rico, rico*," which means "rich". They stopped by the time he was old enough to fight, as he grew rather large as well, but by then the name had stuck. My parents are the only ones who call him Richard.'

'You didn't care for growing tobacco?'

Reid shook his head.

'I don't seem cut out to be a farmer. I went into the Bank of London and South America after college, and eventually progressed to where I am now; a sort of superior dogsbody. To be technical, I assess the feasibility and viability of various investment projects for clients who want large-scale loans in Europe and

Latin America. I was having a preliminary look over a tobacco-growing co-operative near Granada the day I encountered you. On impulse I decided to visit the Alhambra afterwards—and there you were.'

'In a tizz,' said Kit ruefully. She raised an eyebrow. 'Haven't *you* left something out too?'

'If you mean the fair sex—well, yes, I've had my fair share of hectic encounters, I suppose. Enjoyable, if not durable. I even got to the stage of proposing once.'

'What happened?'

'She turned me down.'

'Oh. Bad luck!'

'Not really. I was a bit put out at the time, but my recovery was so immediate I hardly think the relationship could have been classed as deep and meaningful, as you put it.' He sat back and swallowed the remainder of his wine in one draught. 'All this talking is thirsty work. Let's have another bottle.'

'Heavens no; not for me. You go ahead, though, if you want.'

'Half a bottle, then!' Reid smiled with such persuasion that Kit weakened, and consented to just one more glass when the waiter brought more of the delicious, chilled wine, but refused offers of dessert.

'You're convinced I'm a hypochondriac, I know.' Her eyes sparkled at him, darkly blue in her sun-flushed face. 'Nevertheless, since my recent little indisposition I seem to have lost my taste for sweet things.'

He looked at her steadily in silence for a while, then he said quietly,

'Perhaps we should forget the last couple of days and start again with a clean sheet.'

Kit smiled mischievously.

'I rather thought you had me down as a half-witted, malingering shrew!'

Reid threw back his head and laughed, an infectious sound that turned the heads of some of their immediate neighbours. He leaned forward across the table, smiling directly in to her eyes.

'In which case why do you imagine I came out in the *Golondrina* yesterday? I knew you were coming. Carlos and Luis are completely proficient at handling the ketch without my assistance, I assure you.'

Kit drank the rest of her wine hastily, feeling oddly confused, hardly noticing when Reid immediately refilled her glass.

'Are you making overtures of friendship, then?' she asked diffidently.

'Would you be displeased if they were overtures of a different kind?'

'I made a vow yesterday,' said Kit obliquely. 'All I wanted was one opportunity, the merest chance, to embarrass you as much as you did me. I lay awake for quite a while last night dreaming up little situations where I was the victor and you were the vanquished.'

'I find that extremely reassuring,' he said, to her surprise, his eyes slitted to a narrow, assessing gleam. 'After all, Katharine, to feature in a lady's dreams must surely be any red-blooded man's aim.'

'Are you flirting with me?' she demanded.

Reid chuckled.

'I saw you reading a Regency romance; I think the terminology's rubbed off!'

Kit joined in the laughter ruefully, yet feeling suddenly lighthearted, and concluded that it must be the effect of the wine combined with the sunlight of the Costa del Sol.

'You look like a fox,' she said abruptly, her head on one side as she openly studied his face. 'I think you're probably just as cunning, too—a wow in your job.'

He frowned.

'I don't know that I care too much for your description——'

'It's all that red-brown effect,' Kit said analytically. 'Hair, eyebrows, even your skin has a reddish-brown tan. And of course you have yellow eyes. Your hair is cut close like a fox's pelt, too——'

'Enough!' Reid held up a hand. 'My self-esteem is diminishing by the second. Let's talk about you. How come you're so dark and the twins are blonde?'

'They follow Mother. Penry and I are more or less like my father.'

'Penry?'

'My father's name is Henry. In Welsh '*ap*' is a prefix meaning 'son of', like the Scots '*mac*'. Ap-Henry is shortened to Penry, who is eighteen, fairly large and *very* clever, despite any impression he tries to give to the contrary.'

'And you dote on him!' Reid smiled with indulgence.

'Yes,' said Kit, surprised, 'I suppose I do. He's noisy and untidy, and leaves dirty sports clobber all over the place, not to mention the so-called music coming from his record-player in alt at all times. But you're quite right, I am very fond of him.'

'So if Penry had come with you to Spain instead of Charity and Clem you would have had a less worrying holiday?'

'They're no trouble at all,' she said, immediately indignant. 'It's just that they're so decorative and there are two of them. Just one of them wouldn't make the same impact, I suppose. But Reid, please believe me, I've made the trouble myself, the girls have been as good as gold.'

'Then I suggest you leave them to their own devices and get on with your own holiday, Katharine.' Reid's eyes held hers for a moment, then he snapped his fingers and the waiter brought their bill. With a sharp look to ensure Kit left her purse unopened he settled up and escorted her slowly through the rows of prone bodies lying in the sun. He pulled their sunbeds out of the shade and Kit untied her pareu quickly, more than ready to lie down after her unusually large lunch. She took out some sun-oil and rubbed some into her skin, flushing a little when Reid offered to do her back.

'No, thanks, I'm going to lie face up.'

He eyed her quizzically.

'Afraid I'll take advantage of the opportunity?'

'Not afraid—just cautious.' Kit gave him an audacious little smile and settled herself down with a sigh of satisfaction. 'I'm really very happy to be doing nothing, I must admit—a born sybarite, I fear.'

'Didn't you enjoy your boat trip yesterday?'

From beneath almost closed eyelids she noted he was lying on his side, turned towards her. The sunbeds were too close together by a long way, she thought uneasily, and gave a little start as his hand took possession of hers and began to play with her fingers.

'Of course I enjoyed it,' she said, shutting her eyes tightly, 'but I also like doing this, too,' and could have bitten her tongue, as he bent his head and kissed the palm of her hand with a soft laugh, touching his own tongue to her skin.

'We're at one accord, at long last, Katharine.'

'Which is a first! Besides, you know perfectly well what I meant.' Kit gave an experimental little tug to free her hand, but his fingers tightened and she was obliged to leave it where it was. She knew all too well that Reid's eyes were fixed on her face, and her whole body began to suffuse with a warmth that had nothing to do with the sun.

'Tell me, Katharine,' he said softly, 'what other firsts you still have left to experience.'

She stiffened, and stayed silent for some time before answering.

'Well,' she said eventually, 'I've never skied down Everest, or sung *Tosca* at Covent Garden, I suppose, if that's what you mean.'

'You know it isn't.' Reid bit the tip of her little finger very gently.

'I'm well aware of what you meant,' Kit answered him coldly. Her eyes were wide open now behind her dark glasses, fixed on the smooth head which was bent over her hand, his eyes hidden from her. 'Considering no one's had the nerve to broach the subject before, it's amazing how immediately I realised what you had in mind.'

Reid's head lifted and he looked across at her with a cynical gleam that made her recoil as far as was possible with her hand still captive in his.

'Is it a sore point, then?' he asked softly.

'My virginity or my lack of it? Really, Mr Livesey, one must be realistic; I'm twenty-six, after all—do you believe in miracles in this day and age?'

He lay perfectly still, yet some quality in his stillness made it very clear to Kit that the saccharine, reasonable tone of her voice had affected him in some way very deeply.

'One can always hope, Katharine.'

She tugged away her hand sharply, all her pleasure in the afternoon spoiled. There was silence for a while. They both lay unmoving, like effigies on a tomb, the earlier atmosphere of cordiality vanished, apparently unlikely to return, and after a while Kit swung her feet to the ground, thrusting her feet back into her sandals. Reid rose and stood, hands on hips as he watched her tie on her pareu.

'Had enough for today?'

She smiled at him brightly.

'No. I've had enough, period.' She searched in the big white bag, and despite something in Reid's stance that foretold danger, she produced a thousand-peseta note and pressed it into his hand, smiling sweetly.

'For my lunch. I do hate feeling obligated.'

The truce was well and truly over. Reid put out a long brown forefinger and hooked it in the top of her bikini, jerking her negligently against his chest, and keeping her there with a hard, relentless arm clasped around her, to the intense interest of the few sun-worshippers in the vicinity still awake. Kit violently regretted her foolhardiness as she looked up in protest into eyes as cold and hard as agates, her breath coming in agitated gasps as his intention became ominously clear.

'People are looking at us,' she said breathlessly. 'Let me go—now!'

'Not yet,' he said pleasantly, and brought his mouth down hard on hers, altering his grip to hold her head still.

Kit tried to pull away, but his arms tightened and he deepened the kiss, creating an instant erotic havoc that made her struggle wildly, regardless of any onlookers, finally succeeding in pushing him away with a decidedly unladylike shove that left her off balance, just long enough for him to reach out and tuck the money in the warm cleft between her breasts.

'I prefer to pay for my pleasures,' he said evenly, apparently completely unaffected by the incident. 'And after all, I did make it clear it was my treat, and I may say very sincerely that treat is just what it was.'

CHAPTER SIX

THERE is a certain similarity between the symptoms of labyrinthitis and the after-effects of a combination of sun, too much wine and the utter and complete loss of temper and dignity. Katharine's retreat over the hot, slithering sand was unavoidably slow and impeded, rather than the rapidity she longed for with every last cell in her body. Added to her fury was a bitter, unreasoning disappointment which she had no intention of analysing. Uncertain whether she was ill, or merely hung over, she gained the steps to the terrace and fairly stormed the short distance to the path leading up to the apartment building, oblivious of the heat.

Once back in the flat she stripped off her clothes and stood under the shower, eyes tightly shut, deliberately obliterating those few hatefully public moments on the beach from her mind.

She switched off the shower and dried herself briskly, gathering her discarded garments with the idea of washing the experiences of the day away along with some necessary laundry. Wrapping herself in Clem's brief scarlet towelling robe, she collected up the twins' underwear with her own and threw them in the bath with some soap powder and warm water to soak while she dried her hair. Rubbing away violently at the tangled, wet mass, she noticed the thousand-peseta note on the bathroom floor. Her mouth tightening, she picked up the money and returned it to her purse in the bedroom, not allowing herself the dramatic luxury of tearing it up viciously. Money was money. She would buy someone a present with it instead.

She was on her knees swishing underwear around in soapsuds when the door-buzzer sounded. The girls must have forgotten the key, she thought, and flung opened the door, arranging a bright smile on her face.

'You're early——' The smile died a quick death as

Reid Livesey pushed past her into the room and deposited her novel on the bar with a thud. 'Get out!' she said fiercely, holding the door wider.

'Not yet,' he said expressionlessly, and stood foursquare in the middle of the small room, making Kit feel intensely claustrophobic.

'My sisters will be back any minute,' she said coldly, 'and I'm not dressed for entertaining——'

'I wouldn't say that.' With one hand Reid shoved the door shut and with the other he pulled her towards him by the front of her dressing gown, looking down at her with such hostility she quailed.

'Please,' she whispered, her mouth suddenly dry. 'Don't—don't——'

'Don't what?'

'I don't know,' she wailed like a lost child. 'Just—whatever it is you mean to do; please don't!'

His hold slackened and the hot, yellow light in his eyes cooled a little.

'You annoyed me, Katharine; annoyed me intensely.'

'You annoyed me, too.' The corners of Kit's full mouth turned down and she looked up at him from beneath drooping, heavy lids. 'What gave you the right to be so personal?'

Reid wasn't listening. He was staring down at her with a very different expression. Kit wasn't sure she preferred it. She shifted restlessly, trying to free herself, but his hand tightened in the damp terry cloth across her breasts, his other arm sliding round her waist.

'Have you ever seen yourself in a mirror looking like that?' he asked, his voice deeper and rougher than usual.

'I've no idea what you mean.' She looked at him with distaste and tried once more to get away, without success.

'I mean with your mouth sulky and your eyes half shut,' he muttered, closing the minimal space between them.

'Let me go! My hair's dripping.' Kit's impatience was tempered with sheer nerves and to her annoyance she could feel herself beginning to tremble.

'Very erotic, long wet hair. Are you afraid of me?'

'No. I'm cold——'

Reid chuckled softly, his tongue running over his lips as he stared down into her wary eyes.

'I don't believe it. Those sleepy eyes give you the lie.' His stare was mesmerising, and she stayed still in his grasp, caught by it until she pulled herself together with a tremendous effort.

'No,' she said breathlessly, and pushed at the rocklike, unyielding chest. 'Please! God, I was wrong about the fox. You're more like a great cat, playing with me like a mouse!'

'In short, an animal.' The laugh deep down in his throat was one of the least humorous sounds Kit had ever heard. 'Well, give a dog a bad name——'

The game was suddenly over. Reid's mouth was hard on hers, his hands pushing aside the robe, despite her furious resistance. Moaning beneath his relentless mouth, she twisted and turned frantically in his grasp.

'No, you don't. You made a fool of me down on the beach, walking out like that. A lady should leave when the time is right; good manners, you know.' Reid's voice was barely recognisable.

'I give you full permission to turn the tables,' panted Kit, her eyes sleepy no longer, but blazing up into his darkly flushed face. 'You can walk out on me right now. In other words, get out!'

'When I'm ready, madam, and not before.' His eyes gleamed oddly cold as his mouth came down again and the struggle resumed. Gradually Kit could feel her strength beginning to ebb and desperately renewed her efforts to resist the hard, hot mouth that possessed hers so thoroughly she hardly noticed the hands that insinuated beneath her robe until his fingers captured a nipple already sensitised by the friction of the damp towelling. Kit's cry was muffled against his mouth as a red-hot streak of sensation pierced her and her struggles intensified for a moment, then stopped abruptly. Reid picked her up and sat down on the sofa, her unresisting body close in his arms. All the fight seemed to drain away from Kit as Reid's mouth became gentle, moving from her mouth to wander down her throat in slow seduction until his lips replaced the caressing fingers on her taut nipple. Her body arched towards him as his mouth and tongue unhurriedly played with first one nipple, then the other, his hands biting into her ribs as he felt her response. His head came up swiftly and his mouth returned to hers again; long, sweet moments passing in honeyed lack of haste, as his lips flicked over hers with a gossamer touch, finally closing over them until their breathing accelerated to a rate where neither could do more than clutch each other in a desperate sort of amazement at the sensations each had called up in the other. Reid held Kit away from him slightly, staring down into her bemused eyes with a look of disbelief in his own.

Her eyes dropped to his bare chest, and she flushed to think that it was her own frantic fingers that had undone shirt-buttons in such wanton haste, any discomfiture immediately forgotten as Reid pulled her close again and held her head hard against his shoulder, his mouth moving over her hair.

The strident note of the door-buzzer tore them apart, rocketing Kit to her feet as she looked in horror at Reid, who was thrusting his shirt into narrow black trousers with something less than his usual unshakeable poise. She tied the short robe round her swiftly and opened the door to her sunburnt, happy sisters, who apologised profusely as they saw her wet hair.

'Sorry, Kit, we forgot our key . . .' Clem's voice trailed away as she caught sight of Reid lounging casually against the bar.

Giving private thanks to her guardian angel, Kit explained that she and Reid had spent a quiet, restful day at the beach, inwardly appalled at her own hypocrisy.

'But she left her book behind, so I brought it up,' he put in smoothly.

'My goodness, you've both caught the sun more than we have; unusual to see you looking red, Kit.' Charity looked from one to the other with interest.

'Did you have a good time?' asked Kit hurriedly.

'Absolutely marvellous!' Both girls had stars in their eyes. 'It was even better than yesterday.'

'Due no doubt to the lack of our sobering influence.' Reid smiled at them both indulgently, then turned to Kit. 'I'll let you get on with drying your hair, Katharine. My apologies for disturbing you. Goodbye.'

Kit smiled at him stiffly, and Chatty opened the door to let him out.

Both girls immediately pounced on their older sister in glee.

'What have you been up to, you sly thing!' accused Clem, grinning from ear to ear.

Feeling physically sick, Kit smiled weakly.

'Yes,' said Chatty with a knowing smile. 'All that talk about wanting a quiet day on the beach was just a ruse to stay behind with Reid!'

Limp with relief, Kit joined in the laughter, her protests of innocence meeting with a sceptical response.

Charity and Clem made drinks while Kit hurriedly rinsed the underwear in the bath and hung it out on the small retractable line provided. Accepting a glass of orange juice, she listened to an animated account of the day, especially their picnic. Carlos had moored the *Golondrina* at a small secluded beach, and afterwards Bruce and Angus had made them all play cricket.

'They were a bit shy at first,' said Clem, 'but five minutes on that gorgeous boat had them right out of their shell, talking nineteen to the dozen—at least to Carlos. Luis has this habit of getting dumb now and then, just staring at Chatty.' The latter blushed violently but made no protest, saying hardly anything at all, just smiling while Clem gave an account of the day.

'Tonight——' began Clem.

'Tonight,' interrupted Kit firmly, 'I would like to stay in. I had a huge lunch, I'm not in the least hungry, and I'm sure you have an invitation, by the look of you, so you can go off to dinner with the Santanas with my blessing.'

Charity found her tongue.

'But Kit, you can't do that! We do have an invitation, but it's not from Luis and Carlos, and it's for the three of us.' She rummaged in her bag and produced an envelope, giving it to Kit. Inside was a single sheet of thick, white paper with the name 'Milagrita' in flowing gilt copperplate at the top. The message was brief. The Señoritas Vaughan would give the writer much pleasure if they would come to supper that evening at her little apartment over the boutique. With apologies for the short notice, etc., Milagrita Carreras.

Kit stared blankly at the dainty, spiky handwriting, then looked up at the twins.

'When did you get this?'

'Carlos had it this morning when we arrived at the boat,' said Chatty anxiously. 'You will come, Kit, won't you?' She fixed her sister with a look of such piercing hope that Kit was helpless before it.

'Yes, I don't really have much choice,' she said slowly. 'It's much too late to send a refusal at this hour. If I'd known this morning. . . .'

'We never thought for a moment that you'd refuse,' said Clem guiltily, 'or we'd have come back to the beach to tell you.'

Kit pulled herself together.

'No, of course not. Why should you? It's very kind of Señora Carreras. Though why she should do such a thing is rather surprising. What time are we expected?'

'Not until nine-thirty.' The look of painful anxiety receded from Charity's face and Kit felt remorseful. What a gorgon she must seem like to Chatty and Clem—probably their mother would have been far more lenient with them.

'Right,' she said with sudden decision, 'I'll dry my hair and pop down to ring the parents while you two have your bath. No need to get dressed for ages, so we'll have a conference on what to wear when I get back. The lady is very elegant, so it's best foot forward tonight. If I were you I'd wear different outfits—play down the twin angle.'

Her sisters were so relieved at Kit's capitulation they would have painted themselves red, white and blue if so required, and went to sort through their small wardrobes carefully while Kit hastily thrust the hot brush through her half-dry hair and pulled on jeans and sweater to go down to the telephone in the foyer. To her relief her mother was alone at home and able to talk undisturbed while Kit poured out her tale about the Santanas and how most of the twins' time was being spent in their company. Mrs Vaughan heard her out in silence, then calmed Kit down immediately with her usual common sense.

'Thank you for taking your responsibilities so seriously, darling, but on the other hand try to keep a sense of proportion. The idea was a holiday to set you on your feet again, not drive you insane! From what you say the young men seem well intentioned, and if Charity has never been alone with her Luis it doesn't appear that his behaviour is suspect. You'll be home in four days' time, so try to relax, darling, and enjoy yourself as well. As girls go they're not so bad, our twins.'

Kit's money was running out, and after hurried assurances that Mrs Vaughan's ankle was doing quite nicely, and so were her father and Penry, she rang off and returned up to the apartment.

The girls appeared to have everything they owned out on their beds, and were deep in discussion as to the right choice.

'She says "supper", not dinner,' said Chatty, forehead furrowed, 'so she'll hardly expect us formally dressed.'

'When in doubt,' said Kit firmly, 'wear whatever you find most comfortable.'

'Jeans!' they said in unison, laughing at Kit's frown.

Finally Charity wore a full swirling skirt of heavy Prussian blue cotton with its own demure square-necked top, edged with coarse cotton lace. Clem regretfully put aside her own green version of the same outfit and decided on the white dress worn to the dance, then looked in disapproval at Kit, who was taking the dark blue shirtwaister off its hanger.

'Not that one, Kit!'

'Why not—it's comfortable and fairly elegant.'

'But not very exciting.'

'It's hardly the occasion for the red taffeta, surely!'

'Well, no, but as Milagrita owns such a pricey boutique she's bound to be the last word. Have you brought your black linen dress?' Chatty gave her a sly grin. 'After all, Reid might be there.'

The thought had occurred to Kit already. He was the one part of the holiday ignored when pouring out her tale to her mother. She stepped into the black dress Charity suggested and conceded that it looked suitable, its slim severity only slightly mitigated by its deep square neck, and the slit at one side of the skirt, well above one tanned knee. Backless, high-heeled black and gilt sandals, gold hoops in her ears and hair brushed up into a Gibson-girl knot on top of her head, all looked more sophisticated than her usual style, and contrasted vividly with the twins, who were looking very young and appealing. When the eagerly awaited buzz sounded at the door Charity flew to open it to Luis, who had come alone to fetch them this evening, as Carlos was needed at the Florida until a little later, though he expected to be in time for supper.

'I am to have the privilege of escorting all three beautiful ladies this evening,' he said gallantly.

'Enough to make a lesser man quail,' said Clem, grinning, and Luis's white teeth gleamed in response.

'Then I am fortunate not to be one of these lesser men!'

'Your English is so good,' sighed Charity. 'I can't imagine being able to speak Spanish like that.'

'It would be a great pleasure to teach you.' Luis was instantly serious, and Chatty's colour rose. Kit eyed her uneasily. Chatty had blushed more in the short time since meeting Luis than ever before in her whole life. Clem winked at her older sister, and Kit smiled unwillingly, then went on to assure Luis that despite their fragile sandals they were all more than capable of walking the short distance to Milagrita's apartment.

It was a beautiful moonlit evening, and the short walk was enjoyed with pleasure by the three girls as they breathed in the balmy little breeze coming in from the sea, the smell of salt stronger as they descended the long curving causeway to the little quay, where some of the shops were still open. Luis led them to a black-hinged white door between Milagrita's boutique and the leather shop next door, using his own key to let them in and conducting them up a flight of stone steps to the floor above. To their surprise and pleasure the door gave on to a small roof-garden with lamps set haphazardly among orange and laurel trees that stood in wooden tubs painted white to match the wrought-iron patio furniture. Their hostess came to meet them immediately, hands outstretched.

'*Bienvenido*—welcome. We have met already, of course.'

'How kind of you to invite us, Señora Carreras,' said Kit. 'You have met my sisters before—Charity in blue, Clemency in white.'

Milagrita laughed, looking from one to the other in amusement.

'How considerate of you to dress differently, *señoritas*, or I should be lost!'

Charity and Clem were the very embodiment of well brought up young ladies as they greeted their hostess and complimented her warmly on the charm of the small, elevated patio, assuring her they were not cold and would love to stay outside to enjoy the cool evening. They avoided Kit's eye, not needing to communicate the first thing that had struck them both about their hostess. She was wearing jeans! Designer jeans of perfect cut, to be sure, worn with fragile-heeled sandals in the same jade-green as her mouthwatering silk chiffon blouse—nevertheless jeans.

There seemed to be no other guests, and Kit slowly began to relax as Luis handed round drinks before settling himself as near Charity as possible.

Milagrita Carreras was a little older than Kit had thought, but her personality was very warm and welcoming, and it was surprisingly easy to tell her about Mrs Vaughan's untimely accident, also the grave misgivings Kit had felt about coming to Spain alone with the twins. Milagrita was sympathetic. She glanced across at Clem, who was animatedly telling Luis about something he obviously found highly entertaining,

Charity content to look on and smile. The tenderness in his manner with Charity was plain for all to see.

'Luis is smitten,' said Milagrita softly, for Kit's ear only. 'Which does not surprise me—she is very beautiful. But it surprises me how he knows which one is which, even though they are dressed differently.'

'After knowing them for a while it's quite easy. They are quite individual really, though until now they have never felt the need to stress the difference.' Kit sighed.

'You worry, Miss Vaughan.' Milagrita's grey eyes were liquid with sympathy. 'Do not. Luis will do nothing to harm her, I assure you.'

'Oddly enough that has never been my worry. I'm just afraid that Charity will find it hard to forget Luis when she returns home.'

'Perhaps she will not?'

'Señora Carreras——'

'That is very much, how do you say, a mouthful, is it not?' The other woman's perfect teeth gleamed in the lamplight like pearls. 'Will you not say Milagrita?'

'Thank you. My name is Katharine, but I am usually called Kit.'

'Kit? Very short and sweet!' Milagrita laughed suddenly. 'Not like my name, which is not my name at all. I was baptised Maria Pilar, but I was such a sickly baby that my father said it was a miracle I survived and called me Milagrita—little miracle.' She turned to the other group, raising her voice. 'Luis! You are neglecting us, how about another drink for Miss—for Kit, and for me? And you young ladies?'

Neither of the twins had touched their glasses of Sangria, however, and Luis smiled indulgently at them before hastening to attend to Kit and his cousin. Suddenly voices sounded from the stairway, and immediately the tone of the evening altered.

'*Holà*, Milagrita!' Carlos called as he came swiftly through the doorway, crossing to kiss Kit's hand, then his sister's cheek. To Kit's inward confusion he was followed by Reid, who smiled at her lazily before saluting his hostess. Looking away hastily, Kit realised a third man had followed the other on to the patio. As the man came forward slowly the lamplight gleamed on hair that was either silver-grey or ash-blond, contrasting sharply with his shirt and well-cut trousers, both black. He looked very different from Reid in his casual light cords and off-white cashmere, or the two Santanas, dressed in the lightweight linen suits they usually favoured.

The twins' faces were alight with curiosity as Milagrita realised she had an unexpected guest. For a second or two everyone seemed frozen in tableau, Milagrita's knuckles white as she clutched her glass, but otherwise composed as she looked steadily at the newcomer.

'*Holà*, Juan,' she said quietly. 'We speak English tonight, in honour of our guests. Kit, allow me to present Juan Carreras, my brother-in-law. Juan, this is Señorita Katharine Vaughan, and these are her twin sisters, Charity and Clemency.'

'I am overwhelmed,' said Juan Carreras quietly. 'So much beauty at once is dazzling to the unaccustomed eye.'

'Since when was your eye unaccustomed Juan?' laughed Carlos. He eyed his sister with a degree of uncertainty. 'You do not mind us inviting Juan, *querida*? There is enough to eat, I am certain. He checked in at the hotel tonight.'

'Of course not,' said Milagrita casually. 'In fact it makes our numbers even. Reid, *amado*, will you help Luis with the drinks, since poor Carlos was obliged to work this evening?'

Reid shot her an odd look, but agreed pleasantly in his normal unemotional way. Carlos immediately installed himself between Charity and Clemency while Juan Carreras, after a moment's hesitation, seated himself on the cushion-strewn bench beside Kit. Milagrita jumped to her feet and went into the apartment, and seconds later soft background music came through a hidden speaker, easing the slightly tense atmosphere.

'You are on holiday, Miss—Vaughan?' Juan Carreras' accent was stronger, and his English less fluent than the Santanas', but something about him appealed strongly to the more sympathetic side of Kit's nature. His eyes were black and wary above a truly hawklike nose, and his thick hair was definitely silver now that Kit could see it more clearly.

'Yes. We must be in the minority in our country, this is our first visit to Spain,' she said. 'We are enjoying it very much, too, though I think I just might find the heat in high summer a little hard to cope with. It's perfect for me right now.'

'Yet you are as dark as any of my countrywomen.' He glanced swiftly at Milagrita, who was deep in a very animated conversation with Reid. 'Darker by far than my sister-in-law, for instance.'

'Ah, but that is only under the influence of your Spanish sun. In my native Wales I revert to a less interesting pallor.'

'I cannot agree with less interesting,' he protested, smiling. 'But if you are Welsh that accounts for it—a Celt, I think you say.' Juan Carreras' smile was an electrifying affair, lighting up his whole face, transforming it to an astonishing degree. Kit was aware that Milagrita faltered in whatever she was telling Reid, and a furtive glance at the latter caught him looking at her in frowning disapproval. Kit sighed. Putting her foot in it somehow, no doubt, as far as Mr Livesey was concerned. She turned to her companion hurriedly, almost missing his question.

'You sigh, *señorita*, you are sad?' Black eyes searched hers for a moment.

'I was thinking that shortly our holiday must end,' she said quickly. 'Soon I shall be back at work making my small contribution towards ministering to the sick.'

'You are a nurse?'

'A pharmacist. My father diagnoses the problem and I dispense the remedy.' Kit smiled at him gaily. 'So far we have reasonable success.'

Juan looked at her gravely.

'To see such a beautiful smile must be a greater remedy than any medicine.'

Milagrita interrupted them at this point to invite them indoors.

'You must come and eat some supper, Kit. It is so late you will receive a bad impression of Santana hospitality.'

'Do you not mean Carreras hospitality?' put in Juan unexpectedly.

'No, I do not.' Milagrita smiled at him sweetly as she took Kit's arm. 'Carlos had a cold supper sent over from the Florida. You know very well I do not cook.'

He looked back at her without expression.

'It was always a possibility that you might change. Women do.'

Milagrita's smile faltered for an instant.

'I am too set in my ways to change now, I think. Come, Kit.'

Very much aware of hidden currents beneath their little interchange, Kit allowed herself to be led inside, very glad of the younger element, the twins lavish in their appreciation of the apartment's large combination dining and living room, where stark white walls and black leather furniture gave an arresting effect. The colour in the room came from big lamps in honey-coloured alabaster, highlighting the modern pictures on two of the walls and picking up the vivid colours in the rugs on the polished wood floor. A table was set with every kind of cold delicacy imaginable, and after helping themselves everyone sat around eating from plates on their knees, and the informality began to relax the tension so apparent between Milagrita and Juan. At the moment he was chatting to Carlos, while Milagrita sat with the twins and Luis, setting out to put the girls at their ease and make them feel welcome. Kit was relieved, though conscious of a fair amount of tension herself as Reid settled himself on the floor at her feet to eat his meal. He was silent as he disposed of a fair-sized plateful, while Kit's enthusiasm for her rare roast beef and pepper salad waned almost as soon as she began eating.

Reid stood up to take her plate, looking at its contents without comment before taking it away, returning almost immediately with another containing buttered crusty bread and a piece of tempting cheese. Sitting beside Kit on the settee this time, he said softly,

'Now eat that; all of it. I detest seeing people pick at food.'

'I don't, normally,' Kit snapped. 'I had an unusually large lunch——' She stopped short, wishing she'd kept quiet.

He moved closer, the warmth of his bare arm pressed against hers.

'I enjoyed my lunch very much, Katharine,' he said, in a tone low enough to be inaudible to the others. 'Did you?'

'Yes. The crayfish was delicious.' Kit took a bite of her cheese. 'It was your choice of topic afterwards that did very little as an aid to digestion.'

'Just because you thought your virtue in question?'

Kit turned a lambent blue eye on him in mock innocence.

'Oh, I'm sorry—I thought you were referring to virginity! Surely you can't be archaic enough to consider virginity and virtue as the same thing?'

Reid frowned down into the glass he was holding.

'No doubt it's a very chauvinistic attitude, but I must be honest; I think most men do,' he said slowly.

Kit turned on him fiercely.

'I thought so! Then you consider that if a woman slips just once, and that slip costs her this priceless virginity, she may never again be considered virtuous, while the chaste woman with a disposition like vinegar, who's a stranger to kindness and warmth, is irrefutably virtuous in perpetuity!'

Reid threw back his head and laughed, holding up his hand in acknowledgment of defeat.

'Very well, I concede, though somehow I think you've bested me with semantics.'

To Kit's embarrassment the others had broken off their own conversations in surprise at the low-toned but obviously fierce little interchange. She blushed as Carlos grinned and asked if anyone could join in, Luis promising support if Reid needed it, but to Kit's intense relief no one asked what they were actually arguing about. From the speculative looks on the faces of the twins she would have to think up something fairly convincing to satisfy them later.

Kit was caught off guard as Reid bent towards her, and spoke for her ears alone.

'Was everything all right after I left this afternoon, Katharine?'

The colour heightened in her cheeks, and she looked down, studying her fingernails intently.

'Yes. Charity and Clem teased me a little, that's all.'

Reid shot a penetrating look at her downbent head.

'Teased? Had they any idea of what they'd interrupted?'

'No. The teasing was because they pretended to think I'd cried off the boat trip to spend the day on the beach with you.'

His fingers came out to cover hers.

'While nothing could be farther from the truth, could it?'

Katharine cast a sidelong glance up at him, to see he was watching her steadily. She gave a little smile.

'Precisely.'

'I think your sisters are admirable girls, I could get very fond of them, but this afternoon I could have wished them in Jericho when they interrupted our——'
He stopped short.

'Our what?' asked Kit with interest. 'Idyll?'

'Very poetic. The best I could think of was "lovemaking".' Reid raised a quizzical eyebrow.

Kit was very glad that Milagrita rose at that moment to supervise coffee, while the various groups broke up and reformed, with Juan talking to Clem and Carlos crossing to take Reid's place by Kit as he went off to help Milagrita, leaving Luis to his heart's desire, a tête-à-tête with Charity. Reid remained close by Milagrita's side for the rest of the evening, and Kit told herself she was relieved. Entertaining though Carlos was, with a fund of anecdotes on hotel life, Kit felt oddly flat, unable to ignore the fact that Milagrita's hand stayed on Reid's arm the whole time, her brilliant light eyes laughing up into his, her general attitude one of careless intimacy and familiarity.

After a while Carlos sighed, frowning.

'Milagrita is not pleased that I bring Juan tonight.'

Kit was curious.

'Doesn't she like him?'

He hesitated.

'She used to—like him very much. But her marriage to his older brother, Pedro, had been arranged while she was in school.'

Kit turned incredulous eyes on the young Spaniard.

'You still have arranged marriages?'

'Sometimes.' Carlos spread expressive hands and shrugged. 'Who knows? Perhaps it is a better system than one thinks, if the statistics on divorce in other countries are accurate.'

'But surely your religion would have something to do with that, rather than the success rate of Spanish marriages, surely?'

'Possibly.'

Kit looked across at Milagrita, who was gazing up into Reid's face with every appearance of rapt interest.

'I would hate it for myself.'

'Unfortunately, so did Milagrita. Juan wished her to defy everyone and run away with him, but she could not bring herself to hurt our parents, and ended in hurting herself—and Juan. Her marriage with Pedro was a disaster, but a brief one. He died in a street accident after only two years. But by then Milagrita had changed very much.'

'Could they not have made it up afterwards, Milagrita and Juan?' Kit was moved by the sad little story.

'Juan has pride, Señorita Kit—all men do, I think, but some Spaniards have too much, perhaps. He works in Granada these days. At the moment he is on a short working holiday here in Marina Costa.'

'Why here?'

'Did Reid not mention it? Juan is the head of a tobacco-growing co-operative, is that right? He has come down for the weekend to have talks with Reid informally.' Carlos smiled at Kit apologetically. '*Perdone*—I bore you.'

Kit shook her head emphatically.

'Not in the least.' She hesitated. 'And does your sister—does Milagrita like Reid, Carlos?'

He gave her a strange look, then rose to his feet.

'We all like Reid, Señorita Kit. Allow me to refill your glass.'

Feeling she had overstepped some undefined boundary, Kit refused another drink and rose to her feet, Charity and Clem following her lead with commendable promptitude. Milagrita came across the room with every appearance of distress.

'You do not go so soon? It is early yet!' Her smile held genuine warmth, and Kit almost weakened for a moment.

'But Katharine is convalescent, she needs her beauty sleep.' Reid smiled mockingly.

Kit turned the full battery of her own smile on him in return.

'I'm not convalescent any more, but I won't deny the rest!' She turned to her hostess. 'It's been a lovely evening, Milagrita, we appreciate your hospitality very much.'

Milagrita smiled, putting out a hand to take Kit's

'I am sorry that this meeting should take place in my little—hideway, yes? But my parents are in the States until next week, and by then you will be at home, I think.'

Mystified, Kit nodded, then made her farewells, surprised when Juan Carreras also left, accompanying Carlos and Luis as they walked the sisters back to the apartment. Her last view of Reid was with Milagrita's hand in his pulling him indoors as the rest of the party descended the flight of steps to the quay.

Juan chatted courteously with Kit on the way back, asking about her home in Wales, and listening with amusement to an expurgated version of her visit to Granada and the Alhambra. The other four were obviously in great accord and all laughed and talked with ease, like friends of long standing.

'You will come with us on the ketch tomorrow, Kit?' asked Luis as they reached the apartment building.

Kit shook her head.

'Thank you, you're very kind, but I prefer to stay on the beach. Charity and Clem will enjoy it even more without me, I'm sure.'

'Bruce and Angus are coming too,' said Clem swiftly.

'Then you certainly don't need me. Goodnight, everyone.'

With much hand-kissing and repeated thanks, their escorts departed, and the three girls arrived in the apartment in three quite different frames of mind. Charity was silent and dreamy, while Clem was bright and talkative, mainly on the subject of the mysterious Señor Carreras.

Kit hardly knew how to describe her own feelings as she prepared the inevitable pre-bedtime tea. Dreary was the word that sprang to mind.

'We've actually met a Don Juan, at last,' remarked Clem. 'Attractive, in a mature sort of way, wasn't he, Kit?'

'Very. But not for you, my child.'

'I don't see why not. His hair is silvery, but he's not old. In fact he's very sexy.' Clem's eyes danced up at Kit in preparation for the rebuke she knew very well was coming.

'Sexy or not, Clemency Vaughan, I think his interests are centred elsewhere.'

'Oh, come on, Kit, you can't have Reid *and* Juan!'

Kit looked at Clem with distaste.

'I don't *have* Reid, as you so nicely put it, and Juan Carreras is still in love with Milagrita.'

'*Still* in love?' Even Charity's interest was now fully aroused as Kit passed on the story Carlos had told her.

'How sad!' Charity looked almost ready to cry, and Clem regarded her twin with anxiety as she went off to prepare for bed in definitely minor key. Clem turned a troubled face on Kit.

'Do you think the course of love is getting a bit rough, Kit?'

'No. It's just that the finishing post is looming near, silly.'

'I suppose you're right. She's going to be a right little bundle of joy when we start back to college.' Clem finished her tea, and held out her hand for Kit's mug. 'I'll wash these. By the way, what were you and Reid arguing about so violently?'

'Semantics,' said Kit tersely.

'Crumbs!' Clem made a face and departed kitchenwards, popping her head back round the door almost immediately. 'Will Reid be down at the beach tomorrow?'

'He'll be tied up all day, I should think.'

'Who to? Milagrita?' Clem grinned and dodged out of sight again, leaving Kit to stare down moodily at her pink-painted toenails before getting up to prepare for bed. All during the cleansing and toning process she stared at herself in the bathroom mirror, trying to see how she looked with a sulky mouth and drooping eyelids. Half-witted, she thought viciously, and went off to her room, to lie in bed with her mind full of the evening's incidents. If Milagrita still cared for Juan, as Carlos said, she had been at great pains to hide it. All that hanging round Reid could have been to make Juan jealous, of course, on the other hand maybe she just liked doing it. Reid hadn't seemed to object. What man would, if it came to that? Kit objected though, she found. Appalled, she realised she'd suppressed a strong urge to tear Reid away from Milagrita for most of the evening. Which was rather shattering, considering she didn't like him very much—and just as well, too, as he obviously wasn't over-fond of Katharine Vaughan. Tomorrow he would probably be with Juan Carreras, talking bank talk presumably, so she would, at long last, achieve her solitary, peaceful day on the beach, with only a crowd of strangers and Georgette Heyer to keep her company. *Deo gratias!*

Wrong, thought Kit wryly next morning. As she ran down the steps to the sands she could see the McPhersons near her usual spot, or at least four of them. Putting a good face on it, she greeted Morag and Alec cheerfully and commiserated with a wan Elspeth and Catriona on their bad luck. Eventually she prevailed on the older pair to take off somewhere for an hour or two on their own while she kept an eye on the little girls, who were quite content just to lie in the shade for the time being, and even dozed a little once their parents were gone, leaving Kit to get on with her novel in peace.

After a while the peace palled. She looked round her restlessly, irritable with herself. Everywhere people lay in pairs, grilling in the sun, eating, drinking, haggling with the innumerable traders who hawked souvenirs round the beach. Some of the less inhibited were even making love, as far as was possible in the public eye. Kit flinched, and turned towards the restaurant, which was already beginning to fill up—not that she could take the little girls there for a meal when they woke; they still looked a bit fragile and were obviously not fully recovered from their stomach upsets. With a sigh Kit pushed her sunglasses firmly on her nose and forced her mind to concentrate on the printed page, with eventual success. A short while afterwards Catriona and Elspeth stirred and asked shyly if Kit felt like a little walk. She agreed readily, made sure sun-hats were firmly in place and, with a hand in each of hers, the little Scottish girls set off happily towards the jetty, to look out to sea beyond the ever-present fishermen and feel the cool breeze blowing in off the water. Kit let them sit for a while watching passing boats of every description, wondering if one of them was the *Golondrina* with their brothers aboard, then slowly they wandered back to find their parents waiting to take them up to the Florida for a carefully chosen lunch.

Kit refused an offer to accompany them and put on her shirt before having her own lunch at the beach restaurant. Immersed in her book, she ate her usual toasted sandwich and drank her lemonade, then returned to her sunbed and dragged it out of the canopy's shade to do some serious sunbathing. Smoothing more sun-oil over herself as far as she could, she was squinting awkwardly over her shoulder trying to oil her back when the bottle was taken out of her hand and a deep, musical voice said,

'You permit me?' Juan Carreras stood watching her surprised face with a smile on his thin-featured face, his hair gleaming like molten silver in the midday sun.

'Hello! I thought you'd have been up to your ears in business talk by now, Señor Carreras.' Kit smiled warmly and waved him to the other lounger.

'Will you permit me to apply oil to your shoulders?' he asked.

Kit nodded, and he stroked the oil on quickly and impersonally, handing back the flask.

'Reid Livesey has been much occupied this morning,' he said, and sat on the edge of the other mattress, looking out to sea. Milagrita? thought Kit instantly, flushing as Juan seemed to sense what she was thinking and smiled reassuringly. 'The *Golondrina* developed a little engine trouble and he has been repairing it, so I have given him the keys of my room at the Florida to have a bath, and I shall join him for a working lunch in an hour.'

'Oh dear,' said Kit ruefully. 'How have the rest of the crew managed to occupy themselves?'

'All four gentlemen have been eager assistants,' smiled Juan. 'Your little sisters, if I may use so inaccurate a term, have spent the time in Mi—my sister-in-law's boutique.'

'Heavens,' said Kit faintly. 'I hope they're still solvent!'

'By now they are out on the water, so do not worry. May I buy you a drink at the bar?'

'No, thanks, I've just had lunch.' Kit hesitated. 'Perhaps you would like to fetch one for yourself and drink it with me in the sun. With only a little left of our holiday I can't afford to waste any sunbathing time.'

Juan laughed and went off to get a glass of beer and returned to sit beside Kit, who felt a little awkward lying in the sun in her brief jade green bikini with a virtual stranger. She put the thought aside impatiently, aware that yesterday there had been no feeling of strangeness with Reid, whom she hardly knew any better. A thought suddenly struck her.

'Why did Reid have to use your room to have a bath?' she asked curiously.

'He is living on the *Golondrina*,' said Juan, amused. 'Did you not realise?'

Kit shrugged her shoulders.

'I hadn't thought about it. Tell me about Granada, Señor Carreras.'

'Juan, please.'

They spent a pleasant half an hour chatting until Juan looked at his watch and got to his feet. As he said goodbye he said,

'I see Reid has come to collect me.'

Oh dear, thought Kit. How nice. She looked up in the direction of Juan's gaze to see Reid standing up on the terrace staring down at them. She lifted a hand to wave, but something in his attitude made her drop it again. Damn the man!

'Ah, I nearly forgot the purpose of my visit,' said Juan casually. 'Carlos and Luis said that as they have been held up with their boat trip they trust it will not displease you if *las hermanitas* return a little later today; well before dusk, they assure you.'

With a smile and a wave he went off in leisurely fashion to meet the figure that stood in brooding silence, watching them from the terrace. On sudden impulse Kit jumped and blew a kiss to the forbidding onlooker, then settled herself face down on her mattress and gave herself up to the warmth of the sun, firmly consigning Reid Livesey to the devil.

For some perverse reason the afternoon seemed long, and Kit had to be stern with herself to remain on the beach at least until four, when the shops opened. She put on shorts and shirt, stowed away her belongings, then made her way slowly up to the town, deciding to explore farther afield than previously and buy the rest of her presents to take home. She enjoyed browsing through the various gift-shops, crammed as they were with tourist-orientated souvenirs, but eventually she came across a small, more exclusive establishment selling only handbags and wallets, and despite language differences, managed to get a good price on a small elegant handbag in the same shade of grey as the belt they had bought at Milagrita's. Her mother would be pleased with that, she knew. The three of them had spent very little really, and had more money to spare than expected. Enjoying herself, Kit haggled for end-of-season prices on a wallet each for her father and Penry and returned to the apartment flushed with success. As she passed through the foyer the janitor called to her and handed her a note. Kit thanked him, surprised, and tore it open in the lift to find it was from Milagrita, asking Kit to call at the boutique for a drink after her sunbathing. A shower to rid herself of sand, and a swift wriggle into white sailcloth trousers with her jade green sun-top were a matter of moments. She was already wearing white hoops in her ears, and a touch of lipgloss was all she felt necessary before she was on her way back down in the lift.

Curious as to why Milagrita should ask to see her again so soon, Kit walked briskly down the causeway to the quay, enjoying the brilliant sunwashed scene of boats and masts and sails, all singing their own siren song of wind and sea to lure the onlooker. At the boutique a young girl was officiating today, busy with several customers. Kit asked haltingly for Señora Carreras and was waved upwards with sign language. The door at the foot of the outside staircase was open and she slowly climbed the shallow stone steps, to find Milagrita waiting for her at the top, soignée in a coffee-tinted silk dress.

'Kit—how nice of you to come! I thought perhaps you would not.' Milagrita smiled almost nervously and waved Kit to one of the cushioned chairs. 'Something alcoholic or——'

'No, thanks,' said Kit quickly. 'Lemonade would be lovely.'

When the glasses were in front of them on the small white-painted table she smiled politely at her hostess.

'I would have been here earlier, but I had a little shopping spree for presents; my parents and brother.'

'Ah, I see. I thought——' Milagrita hesitated. 'After last night I thought you might not care to come.'

Kit looked at her in surprise.

'But we had a very pleasant evening. . . .'

'I did not.' Something in the short, bitter words touched Kit. She put out a hand and touched Milagrita's.

'Because of Juan Carreras?'

'You know?' The light grey eyes were full of pain.

'Carlos explained a little. I hope you don't mind.'

'No, no. It is more easy for you to understand. I was startled to see Juan unexpectedly, and then I—I behaved very badly, acting as though Reid and I are—involved.' Milagrita looked at Kit in appeal. 'We are not involved in any way, except as friends, please believe me.'

Kit felt decidedly uncomfortable, and stared down into her lemonade.

'It really doesn't concern me at all, Milagrita. And I quite understand.'

'Ah, but it does concern you Kit. Reid is very much, how do you say—attracted to you, I know, yet even so he was too much a—a gentleman to. . . .'

'Repulse any advances of yours?' Kit flashed her a friendly grin.

Milagrita smiled brilliantly in relief.

'*Si*—exactly. I wished to show Juan I did not care. Which is stupid; *loca*! For he thought I did not care enough all those years ago. Even though I did—I do. I always have. It is not my custom to confide in a stranger like this, Kit, but you have little time here now and I thought you should hear what I have to say. My marriage was not happy. Pedro and I—we—well, we were not suited. Some aspects of my life with him were very hard to bear.' Milagrita flushed, twisting the rings on her hands. 'And even though it is over three years since his death, Juan will not—will not——'

To Kit's consternation great tears began to roll down Milagrita's face and splash on the silk of her dress. With a muttered '*perdone*' she fled indoors, and returned five minutes later, red-eyed, but more composed.

'Please don't concern yourself about Reid,' Kit assured her. 'He doesn't really like me all that much, and I have no idea how I feel about him, all of which is quite irrelevant anyway, as on Sunday the twins and I go home and that will be that. I'm afraid it's Charity who will feel it most.'

'Ah yes, but you see, that is the whole point,' said Milagrita earnestly.

Kit looked blank, wondering if she'd missed something somewhere.

'I'm sorry——'

'I behaved badly with Reid last night just to annoy Juan, heedless of whether I hurt you indirectly—no, please,' as Kit started to speak. 'And I do not wish to hurt you for two reasons. One, I like you.' Milagrita smiled disarmingly. 'Second, although Luis is actually my cousin he is more like a brother, because his mother died when he was born, and his father soon afterwards.'

Kit was puzzled, but heard her hostess out.

'Luis has always lived with us; he learn the business with my father and go—no, *went* to college in England like Carlos. He loves your sister.' Kit sat bolt upright, but Milagrita held up her hand. 'Do not worry. He has not said this to her, because my parents are away. He must tell them first. Then he must see *your* parents, and only then will he speak to Charity.'

Kit was stunned.

'I had no idea affairs were still conducted in this formal manner,' she began.

'They are not very often, but this is how we have been brought up, and Luis feels he owes much to my parents.'

'I see,' said Kit slowly. 'But it's not only that. They only met a week ago—I can't believe that it's long enough.'

'It only takes a moment to fall in love,' said Milagrita bleakly. 'I saw Juan first when I was sixteen years old. It was the day I met Pedro too. One I loved, the other I did not, and I have never changed.'

'But Charity is so young!'

'How old?'

'Nearly twenty.'

'We consider that old enough, and more, in Spain.' Milagrita smiled. 'Because you are older yourself you find it difficult to believe one can love deeply at such an early age?'

Kit was quiet for some time.

'No, I don't think so,' she said eventually. 'But in Britain these days the outlook is so different.'

'Is this why you are not married? You do not care for the idea?'

'I've never met anyone I wanted to marry,' said Kit frankly. 'I'm destined to be an old maid, I think!'

'Then it is not that you disapprove of Luis?'

'No, no, of course not. He's a very charming young man. And I admit that I've never seen Charity like this. She's off in some other world most of the time. Clem is worried that she'll be miserable when we leave.'

'Then would it not be better for Luis at least to broach the subject of a longer lasting relationship, then he could come and visit your parents, perhaps after a period of letter-writing, then eventually the passage of time will tell us if their feelings are durable.' Milagrita looked earnestly at Kit. 'I would like Luis to be happy, and you feel the same for your sister, I know.'

Kit put out a hand and clasped Milagrita's.

'Of course. You would like me to put in a good word with my parents.'

'*Si*, that would be marvellous. And now I think I can see the *Golondrina* coming in. Our little ones will soon be with us. Let us go to wave from the edge of the roof.'

As they perched on the low wall, watching the far off activity of the disembarking sailors, Milagrita said delicately,

'You said very little about Reid, Kit. Do you—well, are you attracted to him?'

'Half of me is,' answered Kit honestly. 'The other half is constantly being rubbed the wrong way.'

'What is that?' Milagrita frowned.

'We annoy, anger each other.'

A knowing smile lit up the other woman's face.

'At least you are not indifferent, then!'

'No, indeed—ah, there they are, they've seen us.' Kit waved vigorously, Milagrita joining in.

'*Holà, niños,*' she called.

The look on the twins' faces was comic, obviously taken aback to find Kit in the last place they expected her to be. Kit looked down at the six brown, flushed faces indulgently, her face softening as she saw Luis bend towards Charity, obviously reassuring her that all was well, his attitude fiercely protective at her anxiety on seeing Kit with Milagrita. They were a disreputable bunch, Carlos and Luis in oil-smeared jeans, the McPhersons just as dirty, and Chatty and Clem looked as though they'd been hauling coal.

'My elegant little sisters,' grinned Kit at Milagrita, then she leant over the wall.

'What a lot of ruffians you look—had a good day?'

Charity's face cleared instantly, the radiance of her smile quite undimmed by the streak of oil across her nose.

'Perfect,' she said simply.

CHAPTER SEVEN

'WHAT were you doing at Milagrita's?' demanded Clem as soon as they were alone.

'She sent a note asking me for a drink while I waited for the wanderers' return.' Kit looked at her sister disparagingly. 'Come on, put a move on, you two, I don't know that I care to be seen with two such disreputable characters. All your gear can go straight in the bath as soon as you get out of it. I've had mine.'

'It was great fun,' said Charity, unmoved. 'The engine got a bit temperamental after lunch too, so we all lent a hand.'

'And a nose, too, by the look of yours!' Kit shooed the grubby pair quickly into the lift, glad to get them out of the public eye.

'Bruce and Angus had an absolute ball! It was more fun when the engine went wrong then when it was running perfectly.' Clem giggled as she saw herself in the bedroom mirror. 'I see what you mean, oh, great white chief.'

When two very different creatures emerged from their vigorous scrubbing they came into the living room wrapped in towels to dry their hair. Kit was sprawled inelegantly near the open verandah, her feet on a footstool as she sipped at a glass of sherry and went on with her novel.

'How do you fancy a barbecue tonight, Kit?' Clem looked at her eagerly. 'Luis and Carlos know this place where they have a super bar in a garden by a river with a barbecue and live rock-'n'-roll music. How about it? They've invited the boys, too.'

'How kind they are,' said Kit warmly. 'Nevertheless it doesn't really appeal to me overmuch, if you don't mind. I fancy a nice, peaceful evening here with my book and the cassette player, and you can tell them to send me up a pizza from the Italian restaurant on your way out.'

'Oh, Kit,' sighed Chatty, exasperated, 'you are the end! We're on holiday, for heaven's sake, why won't you come?'

'Because I really don't want to—honestly. I'll be much happier here. I feel a bit lazy, actually, and the thought of changing and going out is too much effort.' Kit smiled reassuringly, but Clem examined her suspiciously.

'Not giddy or sick, or anything, are you? Tell me the truth!'

'I'm perfectly well, but I spent ages at the shops this afternoon, and I merely want to stay home and put my feet up, if it's all the same to you. Go and have fun, and don't be too late.'

Only half convinced, the girls went to get dressed, still protesting at intervals, until Kit was highly thankful to see the back of them as she pushed them through the door to wait for Luis and Carlos in the foyer below.

With a sigh of relief Kit poured herself another sherry, put a tape of Fleetwood Mac on the cassette player and kicked off her sandals to stretch out on the settee with her book. Feeling relaxed and peaceful, genuinely pleased to have an evening to herself, she settled down happily and read for some time, only moving to change over the cassette. When the door buzzer sounded some time later she frowned, then remembered the pizza she'd asked for, hoping Clem had ordered the one with onions and peppers. She opened the door to stare blankly at Reid.

'May I come in?' he asked politely.

'I suppose so.' Kit collected herself and waved him to a chair, closing the door. 'Sherry?'

'Thank you.' Reid accepted his glass, examining her carefully from hair to toenails. 'Aren't you feeling so hot? I met the twins with their male convoy and they said you wanted an evening in, so I thought I'd investigate.'

Kit felt at a decided disadvantage as she eyed her visitor warily. Reid was looking particularly attractive in silvery-beige shirt and cords, a brown wool sweater knotted carelessly round his shoulders by the sleeves. Her own casual outfit and bare brown feet hardly measured up to him.

'How kind of you,' she said, sitting down on the settee.

'Not kind. I wanted to talk to you.' Reid smiled, with a warmth normally missing from his cool hazel eyes. 'Milagrita told me this evening that she'd explained to you about Juan. I was a shade uptight when I saw him down on the beach with you this morning. I thought maybe it was some kind of retaliation after last night— at least I did until you blew me a kiss.'

Kit looked at him thoughtfully.

'I shall have to control these childish impulses.' She shook back her hair. 'Retaliation sounds remarkably petty and immature, hardly a flattering thing to think about me, Reid. For one thing, what you do with Milagrita, or anyone else, is your affair entirely. For another, Juan was merely strolling by on the beach killing time until his appointment with you, also he had a message to give me from the Santanas. I don't quite see how you or I have any grievance.'

'I haven't. Which still made no difference to my getting uptight.'

Kit was uncertain how to take this.

'I'm sorry you were obliged to play Good Samaritan in Granada,' she said, looking away from the probing look Reid was keeping on her face. 'It's bad luck that you don't seem able to avoid running into me ever since, too.'

'Can you honestly say that I've tried?' Reid smiled gently, leaning forward to look into her face.

'No. Now that you come to mention it. Which is strange, considering how we manage to rub each other the wrong way all the time.'

'Not all the time, Katharine.' One long-fingered hand turned her face up to his. 'For a while yesterday I felt that we were completely in tune; very sweetly in tune, I may add.'

For long, immeasurable moments they stayed still, hardly breathing, as though imprisoned in amber. Eventually, with infinite care, Reid drew a long unsteady breath and released Kit's face, sitting back in his chair and emptying the contents of his glass in one swallow. She remained where she was, uncertain how to break the tension that spun between them like the thread from a spindle, taut, palpably quivering.

When Reid spoke his voice was carefully conversational.

'Charity and Clem are happily occupied at some barbecue this evening, I believe. You'll be pleased to hear Milagrita and Juan are dining à deux; apparently enjoying a precarious truce pro tem. Which leaves only you and me. It seems a shame, even wasteful, to spend the evening separately and alone when we could pass the time very pleasantly together.'

'How?'

Kit's single word of response hung in the air for long moments, suspended on the cord of tension that still stretched tight between them.

Suddenly Reid smiled, a cajoling light in his eyes unfamiliar to Kit.

'I thought we could walk a little, talk a lot, and perhaps you would be brave enough to take pot luck with me on board the *Golondrina*.'

She smiled back involuntarily.

'I was going to stay in and be lazy. . . .' she began hesitantly.

He pounced.

'Ah, but your choice of tense shows you've already given in and you're about to accept.'

'Not semantics again!' Kit grinned and jumped to her feet. 'Thank you, I will. Help yourself to sherry while I change.'

'Quite unnecessary.' His unhurried inspection was obviously approving. You look very—satisfactory just the way you are.'

She made a face at him, all constraint gone with the wind.

'If I'm going out with a man I expect to merit a better word than "satisfactory" Mr Livesey.'

'Back to the semantics.' He lifted his glass. 'Move it, then, Katharine.'

Reid was gratifyingly surprised at how soon Kit reappeared wearing narrow black velvet trousers and a silk shirt in a glowing shade of apricot. Gilt sandals, gold earrings and her hair hanging shining and loose and she was ready.

'There—was I quick enough?' she demanded as she rejoined him, slightly out of breath.

He sprang to his feet, and from the unguarded look of admiration on his face obviously felt the wait would have been worthwhile if twice as long.

Going down in the lift Kit suddenly remembered something.

'I ordered a pizza—what will happen to it?'

'I intercepted it as I arrived and donated it to the janitor.'

'So you were quite sure I'd say yes well in advance?'

'Hopeful, rather than sure!'

Laughing, surrendering herself to a sudden feeling of exhilaration, Kit linked her arm through Reid's as they set off for the marina, all the recent tension replaced by a feeling of joyful anticipation.

The lamps strung like crystal beads between the palms along the marina looked pale, delicate in the brilliance of the moonlight that gleamed on the lustre of brass and sheen of mahogany as they boarded the *Golondrina*. All was quiet at this hour, the marina deserted for the eating places of the resort, the only sounds the creaking of hulls and the hiss of rigging, overall the soft lapping of water as Reid handed Kit down on the deck.

'Everyone's out painting the town red at this time of night,' he said in her ear, and led the way below decks.

Kit was oddly surprised when he switched on two small lamps in the bulkheads. Their gold shades shed a soft light over the cabin, enclosing it in an atmospheric isolation that was at once intimate and cosy.

'Where does the electricity come from?' she asked.

'We're plugged in to those bollard-type things on the quayside for electricity, water and even telephone.' Reid smiled at her surprise. 'I'm afraid the outside world is able to contact me at all times, even here.'

He set out two glasses and opened a bottle of wine with a practised flick of the wrist. 'Even so, it's better than the inevitable hotel. Carlos and Luis pressed me to be their guest at the Florida, but I opted for the boat—I get fed up to here with hotel life on occasion.'

Kit looked at the wine in her glass.

'What is this, Reid?'

'An amiable little claret. Having made a start with sherry I thought you'd prefer to stay with wine. It won't do you any harm, I promise.'

He sat down on the bunk, leaning back with his face turned towards her.

'Let's drink a toast,' he said lightly. 'To amity.'

'Amen to that,' agreed Kit, and drank a little of the smooth, mellow wine, a little at a loss for something to say.

'What is it, Katharine? Not shy, surely?'

'Not shy exactly. Plain awkward, I think. This is our first time alone in what one might call an atmosphere of harmony, and I seem to be a little tongue-tied.' Kit smiled at him honestly.

Reid got to his feet and switched on a radio cassette player on a small shelf, inserting a cassette.

'A little background music, perhaps.'

The muted, melodious voice of Johnny Mathis filled the cabin, and Reid returned to sit close to Kit, taking her hand and playing with her fingers absently.

'Better?' he murmured.

Kit leaned back, beginning to relax a little.

'We could be the only people in the world,' she said dreamily, 'encapsulated here in this small space. . . .'

'Would you prefer to go on deck?' Reid's voice was gentle as he clasped her hand in his.

'No. I like it here.' She turned to look at him, her blue eyes shining in the soft light. 'Besides, Mr Livesey, I presume you intend to feed me!'

He sprang to his feet at once, bowing with mock deference.

'Of course, ma'am, at once—but I warn you my scope isn't very great; steaks, salad, fresh fruit and cheese. I did warn you it was pot luck.'

'Sounds tempting to me, just my sort of meal.' Kit followed Reid through to the galley. 'What can I do to help?'

'Lay the table while I start grilling.'

She followed instructions obediently, setting the table with cutlery and plates and striped napkins in blue and yellow to match the curtains. The feeling of intimacy was emphasised as, inevitably, there was the odd slight collision as they prepared the meal, dispelling any last vestige of constraint as Kit put together a bowl of lettuce, tomatoes, onion rings and juicy red peppers.

'*And*, what's more, if you have the ingredients I'll make some dressing,' she promised, growing slightly dishevelled as she worked. Reid had tied a large tea-towel round her waist, and her hair was pushed behind her ears out of the way.

Reid flipped the steaks over then provided her with oil, vinegar, and dry English mustard.

'Fancy you having that,' said Kit in admiration, 'now I just need garlic salt and sugar.'

'Sugar?' Reid grinned, eyebrows raised.

'Yes,' she said firmly. 'Just a teaspoon.' She mixed the ingredients together, poured the result over the salad and tossed energetically, her host so engrossed in watching the process he almost forgot the steaks, which happily were pronounced perfect when they both attacked them with enthusiasm a short time afterwards.

'Gorgeous!' Mouth unashamedly full, Kit nevertheless managed to beam approval at Reid, her eyes wide and sparkling, their sleepy droop missing. 'How do you like the dressing?'

'I'll sign you on as mate any day.' His eyes danced as he filled their glasses. 'No double entendre intended!'

Kit grinned back and tapped a fingernail against her glass.

'Steady on! I have a tendency to drink too much when I'm with you.'

'Are you implying my company is only bearable through a haze of alcohol?'

'Certainly not.' Kit paused in the act of buttering a

crusty roll. 'I'm having fun, Reid. Thank you for asking me.'

'No. Thank *you* for coming.' His face was intent and serious for a moment as he looked at her across the small table, then his eyebrows shot up as he caught sight of her plate. 'My God, you've actually eaten everything in front of you!'

Kit looked down in surprise.

'So I have—and enjoyed it enormously too. I think I can manage some of that cheese I saw, too, please.'

Reid got up promptly and went into the galley, returning with a piece of Stilton and a wedge of Brie, ripely perfect.

'Compliments of the Santanas,' he said, 'They wanted to send across a complete dinner, but I told them it would spoil my fun.'

Kit was thoughtful as she cut herself some Brie. She spread it very carefully on a piece of bread roll and bit into it.

'Did they know I was coming?'

'How could they? I didn't know myself.' Reid sat down close beside Kit. 'Charity and Clem now know I intended to persuade you out for a meal, but I didn't mention the venue.' He turned his head to smile at her. 'I rather think they were pleased.'

'At their age the idea of staying in voluntarily is unthinkable, I suppose. They were very insistent that I went to this barbecue with them, but I thought they would be better on their own, and frankly I wasn't too ecstatic at the idea of live rock'n'roll music either.' Kit pushed her plate away and licked her fingers with a sigh of contentment. 'That was lovely. Now let's wash up.'

'Let your dinner go down first!'

'No, let's get it out of the way.'

'All right, bossy lady.'

Reid began gathering up plates and washed them in the galley while Kit dried them and put them back in their locker. Afterwards she refused his offer of coffee, content to curl up on the bunk with a glass of wine. After a moment's hesitation Reid sat opposite, his long legs stretched out in front of him. With a grin he leaned over and took away the tea-towel still tucked round her waist, and she chuckled, squirming back comfortably against the cushions to enjoy the rest of her wine.

'Milagrita told me she had a little chat with you this afternoon,' he said lazily.

Kit nodded.

'She was at great pains to apologise for—well, for any misapprehension anyone might have had last night.'

'Not anyone, Kit, only you,' he said evenly, not looking at her.

'Yes, well, she explained she was using you as a sort of defence mechanism against Juan; I gather his appearance rather hit her for six.' Kit looked across at him questioningly. 'Do you think they might settle their differences tonight, Reid?'

He shrugged.

'Who knows? I've had dealings with Juan Carreras before in the line of business. Very inflexible, and proud as the devil, and the trouble is, so is Milagrita. Carlos and Luis think the world of her; they're all very close, so when they knew he was booked in at the Florida both of them were determined to play Cupid, though I think their arrows misfired rather.'

'Oh, I wouldn't say that. I don't think he was exactly overjoyed when you stayed behind with Milagrita last night.'

'I stayed exactly five minutes, then went straight to the Florida and waited until Juan came back with the Santanas and put him straight. Compromising a well-bred Spanish lady is not my scene, though I could hardly let her down in public in her own house. Besides, I'm fond of Milagrita. Do you like her?'

'Yes, very much.' Kit watched Reid refilling her glass with a frown. 'Is that another bottle of wine?'

His teeth glinted in his dark face.

'I could hardly give you brandy without coffee! Don't worry, I'll carry you back, if necessary.'

'Heaven forbid!' Kit's eyes were beginning to feel a little heavy, just the same, and she blinked rapidly to clear them. 'Milagrita sprang a bombshell on me today.

She says Luis is completely serious about wanting to marry Chatty—after only a week.'

'Yes, I know.' Reid looked at her searchingly. 'How do *you* feel about it?'

'I hardly know what to think. I thought they were just having a fairly standard holiday romance, of course, but as they are never really alone, as far as I know, I haven't been too worried.'

'How does Charity feel?'

'I'm not sure. I haven't broached the subject, as I gather he hasn't actually proposed yet.' Kit smiled ruefully. 'He wants to tell Milagrita's parents first, and then ours, before he actually asks Chatty. We'll have to stop calling her that,' she added. 'She's talked less and blushed more since she met Luis than during her entire life before.'

'Do you approve, Katharine?'

'Oh, Reid, I don't know. They come from different backgrounds, different cultures, almost. She's halfway through college. Anyway, apart from all this, Charity's my parents' responsibility, not mine. I like Luis very much, and he's so sweet with Chatty, very protective, while *she* wanders round in a perpetual daze.' She sighed, and sipped her wine, looking up with a smile as Reid moved to sit beside her.

'From what you say, Katharine, you've obviously never felt dazed and silent over a man in your life. Hasn't anyone ever caused a ripple in your calm surface?'

Kit was quiet for a time, glad that Reid was unable to see into her mind. She had no intention of letting him know that *he* was the only one ever to disturb her serenity in any way at all. Merely sitting there, a mere hairsbreadth away from her, he posed a greater threat to her peace of mind than the most enthusiastic of embraces from any other man she had ever known. She gazed steadfastly down into her glass, burningly aware that his eyes never moved from her face, and only by the greatest effort of will was she able to prevent her breathing quickening.

'I've known a fair number of men,' she said, with commendable tranquillity, 'but this shattering love at first sight thing is obviously not standard procedure for all and sundry. *I've* certainly never experienced it, and at my age I don't suppose I'm ever likely to.'

Reid took her hand and smiled.

'Oh, I'd say you still had a bit of life left in you yet, Grandma.' He lifted her hands to his lips. 'When we were so rudely interrupted yesterday you were experiencing some sort of reaction, surely?'

Kit stiffened and tried to take her hand away, but he held it firmly.

'I thought we were discussing mental processes, not fairly mechanical physical responses,' she said flatly.

Reid's glinting look of irony was irritating in the extreme, and Kit drank some wine crossly, of the opinion he should have had the grace to ignore that particular incident, forgetting it as completely as she had; well, almost.

'We've managed to pass quite some time tonight before disagreeing,' he said softly, his thumb rubbing rhythmically back and forth on the back of her hand. 'Don't let's spoil it now.'

'*You* spoilt it,' said Kit childishly, refusing to look at him.

'All right, I spoilt it. I'm sorry. Am I forgiven?' The coaxing note in Reid's voice softened her in spite of herself, and when he put out his other hand to turn her face towards him she smiled reluctantly at the mock-penitent expression in his eyes. 'Shall we kiss and make up?'

Kit shook her head emphatically.

'No. We seem to stay more friendly if we stick to conversation; impersonal conversation, that is.'

Reid got up to put another tape in the cassette player and refilled their glasses, then to Kit's alarm he turned off the lights.

'Hey!' she protested instantly. 'Why do that?'

'For one thing the moon is bright enough to read by, and perhaps you might feel less defensive towards me if you can't see me so well.'

I don't need to see you, thought Kit bitterly, just being there is enough. She swung her feet to the floor.

'Time I was going.'

'Not just yet. Finish your wine first.' Reid's hand propelled her back down against the cushions. 'Here's your glass.'

'I don't think I should have any more.' Kit's voice was nervous. 'The twins will be wondering where I am.'

'Nonsense, it's early. They won't be home for hours yet. Relax, Katharine.'

Despite herself Kit was reassured, and she took a sip of wine almost automatically.

'Did you bring me here just to——'

'Leap on you at the first opportunity? No. If that was my sole aim we could have stayed in your apartment.' Reid leaned towards her, his features clearly outlined in the moonlight. 'I wanted the pleasure of your company, Katharine, without the twins, or the Santanas; just the two of us. A fairly normal male instinct where a beautiful, intelligent woman is concerned, surely. When the lady is good company and even domesticated into the bargain, why must I have any other motive for my invitation?'

Reid's voice was all sweet reason, but something in the way he leaned slightly towards her, an indefinable urgency in his body's posture, was at odds with the words he was saying.

'The thought crossed my mind that you might want to take up where you left off yesterday,' muttered Kit.

'I do.'

She stiffened, then relaxed a little as he went on.

'But I won't unless you want me to.' Reid leaned back again.

She was very thoughtful as she finished her drink.

'I did want you to yesterday,' she said honestly. 'But that was yesterday. I felt almost physically sick when the twins arrived and caught us. . . .'

'*In flagrante?*'

'Not precisely. But after all, *I'm* the one who came along on the trip to keep an eye on *them*, and they've behaved in quite exemplary fashion so far, while there was I, old enough to know a great deal better, carrying on like that. I felt distinctly grubby.'

'I see. Which was why you were decidedly frosty last night.'

Kit nodded.

'And apart from that . . .' her voice was so quiet he had to lean close to hear, 'you made love to me as if it were some sort of punishment—against your will.'

Reid gently took her glass away, taking it through to the galley with his own, then he came back and stood looking down at her, a brooding expression on his face easily discernible, despite the dim light.

'Katharine, I'm not angry with you now. Are you angry with me?'

Kit shook her head mutely, her eyes held by his.

'Normally,' he said with obvious care, 'it's a fatal mistake to ask a woman's permission to kiss her. She's duty bound to refuse. Nevertheless you and I, in the short time we've known each other, invariably seem to start off on the wrong foot, so this time you can choose, Katharine. I hope very much you won't, but if you want I shall take you home right now. On the other hand you could stay, let me sit beside you, put my arms around you, exchange a perfectly innocuous kiss or two and round off a very, very pleasant evening. But I leave it to you.'

Kit was on her feet before Reid had finished.

'In that case,' she said coolly, 'it's time I went——'

'Oh, to hell with it!'

The breath was suddenly knocked from her body as he jerked her savagely into his arms and began kissing her with such force she was dizzy.

Lifting his head a little, he stared down into her wide, shocked eyes.

'I tried—I bloody well tried this time, but it's no use. You just don't respond to reason——'

'Reason!' she hissed, struggling vainly to free herself. 'You sounded like the cold-blooded chairman of a meeting. I'm not an item on an agenda!'

'Cold-blooded!' His teeth showed fleetingly in a mirthless smile. 'Oh no, Katharine, I'm not cold-blooded. And whatever you say to the contrary, neither are you.'

He swung her up effortlessly in his arms and sat down with her on the bunk, his mouth stifling the protests she was violently struggling to make. One negligent hand caught both her flailing ones and reduced her to something approaching submission as he kept her hands behind her back. Without warning Reid swung his legs up on the bunk and lay on his back, with Kit captive on top of him as one relentless hand held her head still, her mouth against his. She began to struggle in deadly earnest, kicking and writhing, trying to bring up her knee to halt him as brutally as she could, but with a smothered curse he literally turned the tables, rolling over until it was she who lay on her back with six feet of bone and muscle and sinew fair and square on top of her, effectively putting an end to any further resistance.

Her breath came tearing from her lungs in painful gasps as she lay compressed by what felt like a ton weight. Eyes closed, she stubbornly refused to speak, determined not to plead for escape from this ignominious subjugation. Gradually Reid's breathing slowed, and without his stirring in the slightest some indefinable change occurred in his posture, but still Kit remained blindly shut away within herself, refusing to acknowledge the hateful fact of his physical superiority.

'Kit!'

Hearing him use the diminutive for the first time breached her defences. Tears slid slowly from beneath her lids and gleamed silver in the moonlight. She felt a great shuddering breath go through him.

'Don't cry.' His body vibrated with urgency. 'Please——' His tongue licked at the tears and her eyes opened fully to stare up into his. For long seconds light eyes stared down into dark, then his mouth came down on hers. With a tired little sigh Kit yielded, and some strange miracle of science took place. Although for some reason the weight of his body on hers was no longer insupportable, her breathing became even shallower and faster as his mouth moved gently on hers, instigating responses her own mouth obeyed blindly. When his lips parted, her own followed suit, synchronised by the same flash flood of desire that bathed them both in a heat that increased and intensified with each caress, each touch. With one hand he smoothed back her hair while the other arm slid beneath her to hold her even closer against him. Unnecessarily, as her body was already pushing itself as hard against him as it could. His tongue licked slowly around the contours of her lips, fuelling the fire mounting in them both to an almost unbearable extent. His body trembled against hers, or hers trembled against his, she neither knew nor cared, gasping in the frenzy that threatened to consume her utterly if nothing was done to alleviate it. She felt no outrage, only gratitude, as he stripped off her shirt and bra, his own shirt following them to the deck. For a second or two she was blessedly cooler, then his hands were stroking and smoothing while his mouth slid down her throat to her breasts, reaching her expectant nipples to kiss and tease and nip gently between his teeth, and the flames licked even higher. Relief came as the cool night air suddenly played on her long, slim legs as he stripped away their last covering, then warmth returned as his body covered hers again, naked as her own.

Kit swallowed convulsively, tried to speak, but his mouth silenced her. She forgot what it was she needed to say. She could remember nothing, think of nothing, there was nothing in the world but this searing, satin contact of skin on skin and mouth on mouth. And pain. She gave a hoarse little scream, struggling frantically.

'Please—no stop!' She strained to break free, but Reid held her fast.

'God help me, Kit, I can't!'

Then there was only a maelstrom of struggle that sucked her down in heat and resentment into its very core, with an underlying burning pleasure she denied with every atom of strength in the body that refused to give in to the very last.

It was abruptly over. The turbulence suddenly ceased, and she felt as though her body was in a million pieces she had no idea how to put together again, ever. Reid drew slowly away from her, his breathing gradually slowing to normal.

'You should have told me,' he said, his voice hoarse and bitter.

She turned her head away from the accusation in his eyes.

'I tried at one point, but you wouldn't listen.'

'It was a trifle late by then,' he said carefully. 'Not just for me. Any man at that particular juncture would have found it impossible to stop, even when——'

'Even when I got in such a maidenly panic.'

He winced at her weary sarcasm, and got to his feet to pull on his clothes.

'You have a lot to learn, Katharine. The struggles were very inflammatory. I'll leave you to get dressed— I'll be up on deck.'

'Thank you.'

Kit pulled herself miserably to her feet and made for the loo, effecting what repairs she could in the confined space, unable to face the thought of the light. She put on pants and trousers, searching unsteadily for her bra and wondering why the boat was rocking so much. Stumbling through the galley, she lurched sharply, giving herself a stunning smack in the eye on something attached to the wall. Her cry brought Reid into the cabin like a rocket and he pulled her into his arms, holding her close while she cried bitter salt tears into his shirt.

'What happened?' he demanded, when she was capable of speech. 'Did you fall?'

'I h-hit my eye on something,' she said with difficulty, great sobs still tearing through her body as he tried to quiet her.

'Let me put on the lights.'

'No!' Panic filled her again. 'I'm not dressed.'

'Do you imagine I don't know!' Something wry in his voice struck a chord in Kit's deeply buried sense of humour, and she smiled very faintly against his chest.

'I can manage now,' she said eventually. 'Please go back up on deck. I won't be long.'

Reluctantly he released her and did as she asked. Abandoning the search for her bra, Kit pulled on her

shirt and looked for her sandals, kicked off so
frantically only a short time before. A shudder ran
through her, but she controlled it quickly and searched
in her small gilt purse for a comb, dragging it roughly
through her hair without looking in a mirror, hating the
thought of facing her own reflection, afraid of what she
would see.

Reid was a dark, silent figure, motionless against the
rail as Kit went unsteadily up on deck. In silence they
left the ketch and walked slowly along the concrete
carriage way, its raw new whiteness softened in the
semi-darkness, the moon now nearly gone.
Unfortunately the concrete was wavering up and down
beneath Kit's feet, and her eye was beginning to hurt
abominably. After her second stumble Reid took hold
of her arm firmly.

'You'll be in the water at this rate.' He drew in his
breath sharply. 'Don't cringe away from me, Kit, I
must touch you to this extent, at least, or I'll never get
you back in one piece.'

She would never be in one piece again, thought Kit
bitterly; it was too late for that.

'What time is it?' she asked politely.

Reid looked at the luminous dial of his watch.

'Eleven forty-five precisely. Quite early. I doubt if
your sisters will have returned yet.'

The pain in Kit's head was getting quite vicious, and
she was hideously afraid her eye was beginning to swell.
Despite Reid's grip she wavered, feeling very sick.

'Could you stop for a moment, please? I don't feel
very well.'

She wrenched her hand from Reid's, subsided
abruptly to her knees and threw up her dinner into the
convenient water of the marina, gasping and coughing
miserably, glad of the cool hand that held her forehead,
while his soothing voice murmured comfort.

'I'm so sorry,' she said politely. 'I'm being an
absolute nuisance.'

'Oh, Kit!' Reid's voice choked, suddenly anything but
calm as he held her tightly in his arms, her face pressed
so closely against his chest that she gave a yelp of

anguish as his shirt button bit into her throbbing eye.

'God, what is it?' Reid thrust her at arm's length to examine her anxiously.

'Just my eye,' she said apologetically. 'It caught on your button. Do let's walk on before we meet anyone— people will think I'm drunk!'

'To hell with people—are you able to walk?' Reid firmly took her arm again.

'Oh yes, I'm fine now,' lied Kit brightly. 'I must apologise for being such an awkward guest. The evening's been a complete disaster, I'm afraid.'

'Not for me.'

Reid's voice was terse and she remained silent, closing her mind to his meaning, finding she needed all her energies to put one foot in front of the other.

'I'm so sorry,' she said conversationally, as they reached the quay. 'I'm afraid——'

Whatever Kit was afraid of Reid never found out, for she folded up neatly into his waiting arms, deeply unconscious. He stared down at his limp burden in despair, then looked about him wildly. Not a soul was in sight, and for a moment he experienced unadulterated panic, then common sense returned. Milagrita! Reid strode swiftly to the quayside door of Milagrita's flat, and kept his finger on the bell until irritated sounds of response came from above. With fervent gratitude that she was there, Reid waited impatiently until the door opened a little to reveal Juan's menacing figure, a glimpse of Milagrita's face over his shoulder.

Juan flung the door wide.

'Reid, *amigo*! *Diós—Kit! Que pasa*?' He quickly relieved Reid of his burden and carried her up the steps with Milagrita running up before, sensibly refraining from questions until Kit was laid gently on the bed in the small spare room.

'We had a meal aboard the *Golondrina*,' said Reid briefly, his face ashen beneath the tan. 'She hit her head on the fire extinguisher, I think, I was above decks at the time.'

'Her poor eye,' mourned Milagrita. 'It will be

completely closed, I think, by morning. Juan, put some ice in a handkerchief. Reid, you stay with Kit while I ring the doctor.'

'Will he come out at this time of night?'

'For me? Naturally!' Milagrita flashed Reid a look of surprise and hurried off.

Reid stood looking down at the still figure, his mouth twisted.

'Do not look so tragic, Reid.' Juan came in with the improvised ice-pack and laid it with great care on Kit's swollen eye. 'One presumes that it was not you who gave her this—shiner, I think you say.'

'Only indirectly.' Reid was unaware of the look of surprise the other man gave him, too occupied with holding the ice on Kit's eye, willing her to come round. She lay inert, a rag doll with hair in a tangle, her cheeks wan beneath the tan. The heavy, shadowed lid on her free eye fluttered and opened slowly, looking blankly up at Reid, her eye moving to the figure of Juan standing anxiously behind him. Her hand moved uncertainly to the ice-pack.

'What——' she began faintly.

'Don't try to talk, Katharine,' said Reid softly. 'I brought you to Milagrita and she's ringing the doctor. Don't worry, you'll soon feel better.'

'Twins. . . .' she managed with difficulty.

'I will go and tell them,' said Juan instantly. 'What is the number of the apartment, Reid?'

Milagrita hurried back into the room, her pretty face filled with concern.

'Dr Garcia will be here in ten minutes, Kit—how do you feel, *querida*?'

'Sorry . . .' Kit's eyes filled slowly with tears, which slid slowly from the corners to run down her cheeks.

Milagrita took the ice-pack away and gently blotted the tears with a tissue. She waved Reid and Juan away.

'Go away, both of you. I stay here with Kit. I would like her in something more comfortable, but I think the doctor should see her first.'

Reid stood irresolute by the bed for a moment, staring down sombrely at Kit.

She refused to meet his eyes and he turned away, lips tightening.

'Very well, Milagrita,' he said heavily. 'Perhaps it's better that I go along and see Charity and Clem myself to reassure them.'

'*Si*, that is best. Tell them I take great care of Kit and they may come to see her first thing in the morning.' Milagrita shooed both men from the room and turned back to Kit, who lay unmoving, her eyes closed. '*Pobrecita*,' she said kindly. 'Lie still until the doctor comes, then I will help you undress.'

Dr Garcia shone a light in Kit's eyes, made several tests, asked her a few questions in pedantic English and said she had slight concussion and should rest all the next day. A light diet, no alcohol, no excitement.

'Doctor, I must fly back to England on Sunday,' Kit said agitatedly.

The short, stout little man looked at her sternly.

'Only if you obey my instructions faithfully, *señorita*.'

Kit thanked him, promising to do just as he said, glad to be alone for a minute while Milagrita saw Dr Garcia from the premises. Her head throbbed, her eye felt swollen and tender, her stomach was still churning, not to mention discomfort in other areas she refused to acknowledge. In short, she thought miserably, she was a total wreck. She tried to smile as Milagrita came back with a white cotton nightdress over her arm.

'Can you stand up, Kit? If I help you to the bathroom, can you manage to freshen up without any help? If not I will wash you.'

Assuring her she could manage, Kit swung her legs slowly over the side of the bed and with Milagrita's support got unsteadily to her feet. Gaining confidence, she managed the short distance to the bathroom without too much trouble.

'Will you be all right, *querida*?'

Milagrita looked a trifle taken aback at the vehemence of Kit's assurance, but only smiled and went off to make tea, telling her unexpected guest not to stay too long in the bath, and to leave the door unlocked in case she felt faint again.

Kit took off her clothes as quickly as possible, and stepped shakily into the warm scented water Milagrita had run for her. Privacy had been essential for various reasons. Swallowing a sob, she bathed as quickly as she could, appalled to see bruises on her arms and various other places they had no right to be. They were not as apparent as they might have been, owing to her tan, but they were unmistakable, nevertheless, and the brief ribbon-trimmed nightdress did little to conceal them. When she plucked up enough courage to look at her face in the mirror Kit gasped in horror. Her eye was almost completely shut, the puffy swollen skin already giving a Technicolor forecast of what it would be next day.

Milagrita appeared, to find Kit slowly returning to bed, and helped her into its welcoming softness, stacking pillows efficiently behind her against the wicker headboard before going off to fetch the tea. She came back with a tray, setting it down on the little glass-topped bedside table, poured tea for Kit, then settled herself at the foot of the bed with a cup of coffee. She looked critically at the other girl's battered appearance.

'What happened, Kit?'

'I had dinner with Reid on board the *Golondrina*, and afterwards I fell and hit my head on the fire extinguisher, I think.' Kit managed a twisted little grin. 'I distinguished myself by being disgustingly sick when we were coming back along the marina, and finally I passed out altogether, I suppose. I'm very sorry it was necessary to disturb you.'

'Nonsense. Reid did the best thing to bring you here—though he startled me much by keeping his hand on the bell. Juan was ready to hit him!'

'Oh dear!—Juan.' Kit looked apologetically at her hostess. 'I ruined your evening as well as Reid's.'

Milagrita's smile was warmly reassuring.

'You interrupted nothing. We are good friends again, Juan and I, at least. He is proud—I think you say "stiff-necked". It will have to be a very gradual process to reach the relationship we once had. He still loves me, I think, but I have to gain his trust again.' She sighed. 'I hope it does not take too long. Life is too short to waste.'

She took Kit's empty cup and put it down on the tray.

'And now I think you should try to sleep. It must have been a bad fall—you have bruises on your arms, I see. Ah, I think I hear Reid returning, so I will leave you now. *Buenas noches*, Kit.'

'Goodnight, Milagrita,' said Kit huskily. 'Thank you once again for your kindness.'

'*No hay de que*. Sleep well.'

The door closed softly and Kit turned to switch off the pink-shaded bedside lamp. She lay staring into the darkness for a long time, painfully aware of the throb in her head; even more acutely aware of the events of the evening. If only the blow to her head had been harder—when she remembered what had happened on board the ketch the idea of amnesia seemed very attractive. She could hear voices very faintly from somewhere in the apartment and wondered if Reid and Juan were still here. She stared into the darkness, worried about the twins, worried about the flight home, and, above all, worried about another eventuality which she refused even to consider, closing her mind to it firmly and deliberately willing herself to sleep. . . .

It was early next morning when Milagrita noiselessly opened the bedroom door, then came in, smiling as she saw Kit was awake. Already bandbox-fresh in white linen trousers and red-dotted white shirt, she made Kit doubly aware of her own untidiness.

'How are you this morning, *querida*? Did you manage to sleep?'

Kit nodded carefully, smiling.

'I feel much better. The head has stopped thumping and I don't feel queasy any more.'

'Queasy? What is that?'

'Sick. Nauseated.'

Milagrita beamed.

'That is good. And now I shall bring you some more of your tea, and perhaps you will eat something. I think you will feel much better if you do.'

Agreeing to the proposed toast and honey, Kit walked warily to the bathroom, but no giddiness threatened, and she availed herself thankfully of the cellophane-wrapped toothbrush thoughtfully provided, after which she very gingerly washed her face. Her reflection was startling. The swelling on her eye had subsided considerably, but this was compensated by an eyelid in a vivid shade of plum, balanced by a very puffy area under the eye in virulent purple shading to a sickly green. Kit breathed deeply and sensibly resisted the urge to burst into tears. No more tears, she decided briskly, and if I do look like a survivor from a dockland brawl—so what?

Her breakfast was waiting when she got back to the bedroom, with the bed neatly made and the pink and white striped curtains drawn back a little to reveal a blue and gold day glittering outside.

'Do not worry,' said Milagrita, as she helped Kit into bed. 'No one can see in through the plants on the patio, and you have a pleasant outlook, as the doctor says you must not get up until this evening, or you won't be fit to travel tomorrow.'

Kit was remorseful.

'But I can't stay here all day, Milagrita! I've put you out enough as it is. I'm very, very grateful, but——'

'Listen, *querida*. I think of Luis, also. If you stay here he can spend his last day with Charity—and Carlos and Clemency, too, of course. But if you go back to the apartment your sisters will insist on staying with you, *no*?'

'But you have the shop——'

'I have a girl to help me, and I can look in now and then to see if it is busy and still keep an eye on you! Now eat your breakfast.'

Kit gave in, making no more protest, secretly relieved that it was unnecessary to move for the time being. Milagrita fetched her own breakfast tray and chatted lightly while they ate. She was obviously curious as to the evening before, but good manners prevented her from asking any questions, to Kit's relief, and before the meal was finished the doorbell rang.

Milagrita jumped to her feet, glancing at her watch.

'Not yet eight; someone is early.'

Kit listened in sudden alarm as the sound of a male voice mingled with Milagrita's, relieved to realise they were speaking Spanish, but to her surprise it was Reid who came into the room after knocking, not Juan.

A look of shock passed involuntarily over his face before it regained its habitual composure, and the look in Reid's eyes was hard to read as he stood at the foot of the bed looking at Kit as she lay against the piled-up pillows.

'Hello, Katharine. How are you this morning? That's a gaudy colour-scheme you're wearing round your eye; not quite in your usual faultless taste.'

'What everyone's wearing this autumn, I assure you.' Kit smiled at him gamely. 'I feel a lot better today; ready to apologise properly for causing such havoc last night.'

'I should be the one to apologise——' he began harshly, but she held up her hand instantly.

'No, don't. Let's forget about last night. Write it off completely.'

'Is that what you want?' His face was bleak, and Kit looked down miserably at her fingers, which were pleating the sheet with great industry.

'I should think it was the only practical point of view,' she said reasonably, keeping her voice steady with effort. 'As the song says, it was just one of those things. I'm going home tomorrow. Soon we'll be able to look back on my eventful little holiday and laugh over it.'

'I'm glad you think so.' Reid came to the side of the bed and sat down, taking her unwilling hand in his. 'I would give anything in the world——'

Kit began to breathe quickly, wishing desperately he would go and leave her to her misery and embarrassment. The word shame was old-fashioned, she thought bitterly. She smiled at him with a sort of febrile gaiety.

'Don't think about it—please. I shan't, I assure you.'

'How the hell am I suppose to go along with that?' Reid flushed angrily, frowning blackly down at their clasped hands. 'I've never been in the same situation before; my experiences with the opposite sex have been solely with women who knew the score.'

'Please!' Kit wrenched her hand away from his and turned her head away blindly. 'You—well, you could hardly have expected. . . . oh lord, you know very well what I mean! Could we just drop it?'

Reid got up immediately, his eyes sombre on her averted face.

'Ignorance is not exoneration. Nevertheless I shall leave you in peace, Katharine, as this is what you want.' He waited a little, but she made no move, and he went to the door, turning to look at her again. 'I'll be somewhere around all day if you need anything.'

Kit turned her head a trifle and met his eyes squarely for the first time.

'Quite unnecessary, Reid, really; I'm in perfectly good hands—now.'

The last quiet, cruel little word seemed to hover in the air for long moments before Reid turned abruptly and went through the door, closing it with a decisive click.

Kit subsided limply, releasing the iron control she had kept clamped down on her emotions. Tears slid weakly from beneath her closed lids, and for a little while she let them fall, until their salt stung her puffy eye and she pulled herself together determinedly, mopping herself with a tissue. She was quite composed when only a few minutes later the sound of familiar voices heralded the arrival of Charity and Clem, who followed Milagrita through the door, stopping short in their tracks as they caught sight of their battered sister.

'Now do not stay too long and tire her,' said Milagrita kindly. 'The doctor said she must rest, or she will not be able to travel tomorrow.'

'Oh Kit, love, what on earth did you manage to do!' Clem went down on her knees by the bed, putting her arms round her sister, while Charity sat on the edge of the bed and held one of Kit's hands clasped tightly between her own.

'Steady on!' Kit tried to keep her laugh unconcerned

as the two anxious faces scanned hers in dismay. 'I know I look like a Hammer film extra, but please don't squeeze me so tight, Clem; I also have a great many bruises elsewhere, and you seem to be finding every one with uncanny accuracy.'

Clem released her instantly and sat back on her heels.

'You must have had quite an evening, Katharine Vaughan,' said Charity severely. 'We left you to a book and an early night, so we didn't even look in your bedroom when we got home in case you were asleep. Imagine the shock we had when Reid appeared!' She frowned at Kit. 'He looked utterly shattered.'

Kit laughed lightly.

'He had to carry me the last bit to Milagrita's; enough to finish a lesser man.'

'Hm.' Chatty was sceptical, but after intercepting a fleeting glance from Clem gave up her probing.

'I thought Reid met you and mentioned he was on his way to invite me to dinner?' Kit looked from one to the other.

'Well, yes,' admitted Clem. 'But somehow we never thought you'd accept!'

Kit changed the subject hurriedly.

'And what about you two, did you have a good time last night?'

'We certainly did—it was great! But never mind that, Milagrita says we're not to bother you with questions, and that you must stay here today.' Charity looked anxious. 'Are you sure you want to?'

Both faces looked so worried Kit felt a pang.

'Don't worry, children, I merely fell and hit my eye on a fire extinguisher. No need for panic. And if I stay here Milagrita says she'll keep an eye on me; totally unnecessary, but very kind, whereas if I come back to the apartment you two will feel constrained to stay with me, driving me mad, instead of spending the last day of your holiday with Luis and Carlos.' Kit kept her voice matter-of-fact and practical, smiling her reassurance. 'But before you set off for the day please fetch me some clothes, something with sleeves, then off you go and enjoy yourselves. You can look in when you get back.'

After a few tiring moments of argument and doubts Kit eventually won the day by telling her sisters bluntly they were making her feel worse than her injuries. They left reluctantly, and Kit sank back into her pillows, more washed out than she cared to acknowledge. The prospect of the flight home next day was daunting at the moment, and she closed her eyes wearily, only to see vivid pictures of the evening before dancing remorselessly behind the closed lids. She opened her eyes despairingly to see Milagrita standing at the foot of the bed, regarding her sympathetically.

'The *niñas*—they are affectionate, but exhausting, yes?'

'Yes!' Kit gave a rueful little smile. 'I had great difficulty in persuading them to leave me for the day. I'm grateful for your hospitality, Milagrita; they would have given me absolutely no peace back in the apartment. My life would have been made hideous with bed-tidying and offers of tea all day.'

Milagrita chuckled, nodding in agreement.

'They are much better out in the *Golondrina*, leaving you in peace. Now, I shall bring you a tray with lemonade and biscuits, some new paperbacks from the shop below and then I leave you alone until lunchtime. *De acuerdo?*'

'Lovely!' Kit smiled appreciatively. She craved solitude, despite the fact that her thoughts were unlikely to be pleasant company. The facts had to be faced and now was as good a time as any.

'Milagrita returned with a tempting tray, as promised with a crystal pitcher of lemonade floating with ice-cubes and slices of fruit, a plate of sugary little biscuits, and a copy of M. M. Kaye's *Trade Winds*, also the latest edition of *Harpers & Queen*.

'There.' Milagrita prepared to depart. 'Now I must open up the boutique and stay there until Dolores arrives at eleven. I shall come up later to check up on you.'

For a while Kit was occupied quite contentedly with the magazine, but after a while her eye began to protest a little, and she slid further down in the bed, prepared to sleep if possible. It was not. The moment her lids drooped the same images flashed behind them in hideously accurate detail, every moment of her encounter with Reid faithfully reproduced. Kit let the mental video film run its length, with no attempt to blot out any part of the proceedings, facing the reality of her seduction squarely, acknowledging baldly that it could all have been averted with a short, clarifying statement early on in the proceedings. Reid would have needed only the slightest of deterrents, she knew. He was no rapist. It was she who was at fault, her own crass stupidity the main element to blame. She flushed painfully with embarrassment at the thought of how astonished Reid must have been.

Firmly she put that thought from her. Tomorrow she would be home again and this whole disastrous incident would soon be history; forgotten. With determination she made her body relax and to her relief eventually it obeyed, the images in her mind finally switching off. Kit drowsed, then slept, comfortable against her nest of pillows, sleeping the morning through unaware of the twins' return with her clothes, or of the man who stood just within the silently opened door, looking at the sleeping girl with a bleak expression in the eyes that showed pale in his darkly tanned face.

To her surprise it was early afternoon when Kit woke, feeling wonderfully refreshed, and looking a great deal different from the girl who had arrived in such a sorry state the night before, as Milagrita informed her gaily when she came to find her visitor awake.

'At last you wake up. It is siesta time for the boutique, so we will have a little *almuerzo, no*?'

'Milagrita, I'm sure I'm a nuisance,' said Kit with contrition. 'I feel so guilty sleeping like that. Though I must admit I feel a lot different after it.'

'You look different too. I must be truthful and say your eye is still a thing of wondrous colour,' smiled Milagrita, 'but otherwise you are a different girl.'

How true, thought Kit wryly, as she threw back the sheet. She swung her feet cautiously to the floor, to the other girl's strong disapproval as she rushed to help.

'I'm fine, truly.' Kit smiled with triumph and stood

up straight, with no trace of vertigo. 'See? Look—no hands!' She was penitent as Milagrita looked blank. 'I mean I'm perfectly well. Did the twins bring me something to wear?'

'Ah, *si*. But I would not let them disturb you. I will fetch your *maleta*, then we shall eat on the patio, yes?'

'Yes, indeed.'

In a very short time Kit was washed and dressed in a flower-printed dress in pink Liberty cotton, her bruises discreetly hidden by its long full sleeves. With her eye concealed behind the large lenses of her sunglasses, white-framed to match the hoops in her ears, she felt ready to face the world.

Milagrita had prepared a large Spanish omelette, which they ate with a tomato salad and washed down with coffee, after Kit's firm refusal of wine.

'After last night I think I'll give up alcohol,' she said, savouring the delicious omelette.

'You did not drink very much, I am sure.' Milagrita eyed her curiously. 'Reid said you had only wine.'

Kit explained about her illness just before the holiday, and how it had possibly made some difference.

'I think my alcohol threshold must be practically nil at the moment, besides. . . .' She trailed away, avoiding the other girl's understanding eyes.

'Besides which you had a disagreement with Reid, I think. He was—very distressed. Too much so for just a fall, which was, after all, just an accident, yes?'

'Yes, of course!' Kit was horrified that Milagrita might think otherwise. 'Reid was up on deck while I tidied myself before going home, and I tripped or something, and gave my eye an extremely violent crack. Utterly stupid thing to do, but certainly no fault of Reid's.'

Milagrita looked thoughtful as she poured coffee.

'Nevertheless I think he feels much to blame, *querida*. He has been back to see you again. I let him come up alone as I was busy, but you were sleeping, he said.' She looked at Kit, a question in her big, light eyes. 'Were you?'

Kit flushed, glad of the dark glasses.

'I was, truly. Was he here long?'

'A few minutes only. He and Juan are lunching together—business again before Reid returns to London. You live near London?'

'No, a long way off. I'm not a city girl; strictly a country bumpkin.'

It took a little time to explain the last, after which, to Kit's relief, the subject of her mishap appeared to be forgotten. They sat talking companionably under the gaily-coloured umbrella, enjoying the sunshine and the activity of the marina until it was time for the boutique to open. Milagrita went off to effect some repairs to her make-up while Kit gathered together the lunch dishes and carried them through to the small, compact little kitchen, where everything was gleaming and in perfect order.

'Leave those,' called Milagrita imperiously. 'I can do them later.'

Kit blithely ignored her and quickly washed the plates. When her hostess reappeared wrathfully all traces of lunch were wiped away.

'You will be ill again,' said Milagrita disapprovingly.

'Rubbish! Two glasses and plates won't kill me—and you keep the place so beautifully it would be a shame to leave things around.'

'*I* don't, *querida*; my maid Concha does that!' Milagrita's eyes twinkled as she prepared to depart. 'It is her weekend off.'

Kit laughed and returned to the guestroom to strip the bed and restore the little room to its former neatness. After this she was heartily glad to stretch out on a lounger under an umbrella on the patio, concentrating on the book Milagrita had brought her, despite certain adventures of the forceful heroine that bore a decided resemblance to her own experience. Nevertheless her morning's sleep had proved to be a powerful restorative and all ill effects from her slight concussion seemed to have gone, to her relief. Milagrita was kept occupied in the boutique, and Kit spent a quiet hour alone before she noticed that the *Golondrina* was once again at its mooring. Shortly afterwards the blonde heads of her sisters came into view, followed by Bruce and Angus's sandy mops and the glossy brown hair of the Santanas as the sextet wandered towards the quay, the McPhersons taking their leave as the other four headed for Milagrita's outer staircase. The twins' faces lit up as they came up on to the patio and saw Kit fully dressed and obviously much recovered. Carlos and Luis came quickly to kiss Kit's hand, while her sisters were voluble in their relief.

'Thank goodness you're better, Kit—different altogether from this morning,' said Clem.

'You didn't look well at all,' agreed Charity, examining Kit's face carefully, 'but one can hardly tell now with the eye hidden.'

'We are very happy to see you recovered, Kit,' said Luis sincerely, drawing up chairs for the twins. 'Charity and Clem were very, very distressed.'

'As were we all,' added Carlos, 'though we are curious to know what the now famous eye looks like behind your sunglasses.'

Kit promptly took them off, laughing at the horror on the young men's faces. She replaced the glasses quickly.

'There! That's enough of that. It will soon go down and no one can see it behind these. I had a marvellous sleep this morning, then Milagrita made a delicious lunch, and frankly, after all this spoiling I don't know how I'll ever settle down to work again at home!'

Charity's face sobered instantly, as did that of Luis, and Kit noted how his hand went out to grasp her sister's tightly, obviously painfully aware of how short a time they had left to spend together.

'I don't think Dad will allow you to go back to work just yet, Kit,' said Clem. 'Personally I think that last night's episode was because you're not entirely recovered.'

Kit denied this stoutly, pressing for details of their day to change the subject. Today's trip had been tempered by sadness for the fact that it was the last.

'But only for the time being,' said Carlos, glancing slyly at Luis. 'I am sure there will be other times. You will come to Marina Costa again, Señorita Kit? You have enjoyed your holiday?'

'Immensely,' she said warmly, keeping any reservations to herself. 'And I'm sure Charity and Clem have never had such a super time.'

'No, never,' they said simultaneously, provoking the usual laughter at their fervent duet.

'However, Kit,' said Luis earnestly, 'it is not over yet; there is still tonight.'

'Ah. Now come what may, tonight really *is* the night I'm going to stay in with a good book. I really can't afford to jeopardise returning home tomorrow.' Kit was adamant, and not all the persuasion of her sisters and Luis and Carlos could move her from her stand, despite the lure of the dinner-dance at the Florida to sway her decision.

'What a noise—and poor Señorita Kit is trying to recover from an outsize headache! How can she, when you *niños del diablo* are making such a *ruido* we could hear you down on the marina!'

Juan Carreras stood smiling goodnaturedly at the fiercely vocal group, and behind him stood Reid, his eyes on Kit. While the others answered Juan's teasing Reid came swiftly to Kit and sat beside her on the chair vacated by Clem.

'How are you feeling?' he asked quietly.

'Fit as a fiddle.' Kit smiled from the shelter of the dark lenses. 'Quite embarrassed at the upset I caused, that's all.'

'I would like to see you alone, Katharine.' The intent hazel-yellow eyes seemed to bore holes in hers, and she looked down hurriedly, shaking her head.

'I don't think I'm fit enough for that,' she murmured.

'Please. Let me give you dinner tonight——' he said urgently, but Clem chipped in cheekily,

'If you're asking her to dinner, Reid, you're out of luck. She insists on staying in, which is the reason for all this argument. We want her to come to the dance at the Florida.'

Reid shook his head instinctively.

'I should think a crowded dance-floor and loud music is the last thing needed after concussion, Clem.'

'Agreed,' said Juan. 'Why do you and Kit not dine with Milagrita and myself at Antonio's; good cuisine, quiet, elegant.'

'And expensive,' grinned Carlos. 'Much better at the Florida.'

Milagrita reappeared, demanding to know why the invalid was being disturbed by so many people talking at once, the younger four immediately telling her why all at once. She clapped her hands over her ears, imploring them to stop, asking Kit how she was surviving such ill treatment.

'Reasonably well,' Kit smiled, avoiding Reid's eye with care, inwardly dismayed at how burningly conscious she was of his proximity. 'My little darlings want me to dine and dance at the Florida——'

'Dance!' ejaculated Milagrita.

'Reid wants her to himself——' put in Luis with a grin.

'And I suggested you and I make up a foursome at Antonio's.' Juan eyed Milagrita warily. She looked back steadily for a moment, then turned to Kit.

'And you, *querida*—what do you want?'

'An evening alone with a book. I intended that last night, and look what happened when I changed my mind. Tonight I really *will* stay in the flat—alone.'

There was an awkward little silence with everyone studiously looking anywhere but at Reid, whose face was as still and blank as a mask carved from wood. Without looking at Kit he rose to his feet.

'There you are, Milagrita, the decision of Solomon. The children go to their dance, you and Juan dine together—uninterrupted tonight, we trust, while Katharine and I spend our evening in private, but separate, pursuits. *Hasta mañana.*' With a casual salute he sauntered over to the stairs and descended unhurriedly to the quay.

'Kit!' Both Clem and Charity rounded on her in reproval. 'How could you be so rude!'

'Not rude,' said Kit, smiling carelessly despite an overwhelming desire to cry. 'Just truthful.'

'Which usually amounts to the same thing,' said Clem, frowning. 'I can't help feeling Mother would disapprove, especially after all the trouble Reid took last night—making tea for us because we were upset, and staying with us until he was sure we were all right. Really, Kit, you're the end, sometimes!'

Milagrita intervened swiftly, noting Kit's colourless face.

'Enough now! You girls can go back and get ready for the evening. Kit can stay here for a while. Juan and I will bring her back later.'

Kit smiled at her dumbly, deeply grateful, and in a short while the patio was peaceful once more, as Juan departed to mix drinks, leaving her alone with Milagrita.

'Something is wrong, Kit,' said the latter gently, and sat near Kit's lounger. 'You were not kind to Reid, and I feel this is not customary for you. Has he offended you in some way?'

Kit had herself well in hand by this time.

'I was a little direct, perhaps. But the desire for a peaceful, solitary evening isn't so terrible, in the circumstances.'

'No, but Reid was obviously disturbed, despite that wooden face he hides behind.' Milagrita examined her perfect oval fingernails with interest. 'I think he cares for you.'

Kit moved restlessly.

'No way. I've been nothing but a nuisance from the moment he was saddled with me in Granada—and he's taken pains to let me know it.'

Milagrita looked up with a smile as Juan came back with a tray laden with glasses, a jug of Sangria and some soft drinks.

'*Gracias*, Juan. Kit, what will you have?'

Accepting a tonic water, Kit drank in pensive silence while Juan and Milagrita exchanged pleasantries.

'I think it would be best if I went along and joined the girls now,' she said eventually. 'I'll leave you to your dinner at Antonio's—heaven knows you deserve it, Milagrita, after a day coping with your boutique and a stray invalid.'

The other girl shrugged her shoulders, grey eyes dancing.

'I am not called "Little Miracle" for nothing, *querida*.' She put her hand on Kit's arm. 'Seriously, it was no trouble, Kit. I wish you and Reid were coming with us, but you know best. What time do you leave tomorrow?'

Kit stood up and set down her glass.

'The flight is at three, so I expect somewhere around one. I expect Luis, or Carlos, will be driving us to Malaga.'

Juan took her arm.

'We will walk back to the Teresa and see you safely to your door; no more accidents, Señorita Vaughan! Come, Milagrita.'

With exaggerated formality he ushered her down the stone steps, Kit picking her way with care as Milagrita brought up the rear with a flood of injunctions to be careful. Kit looked along the marina to the *Golondrina*, bobbing gently at her mooring in the glow of the setting sun, then she turned her back on it, and arm in arm with her watchful companions made her way back the short distance to the apartment building, feeling as though a whole lifetime had elapsed in the twenty-four hours since she had left it.

CHAPTER EIGHT

KIT settled back into life at the medical practice suprisingly well. Her father insisted on a further week at home after the holiday, and Kit agreed, partly because her mother needed help to get Charity and Clem ready for college, and partly because she drew the line at greeting the public with such a conversation-opener of an eye. Angharad Vaughan listened to her three daughters with deep interest as they all talked enthusiastically about the holiday, but her eyes stayed longest on her firstborn's determinedly animated face. Dr Vaughan expressed concern about the black eye, but otherwise said little about Kit's appearance, keeping his views on her well-being for his wife's ear in the privacy of their room.

It was left to Penry to state the obvious in his usual blunt fashion. Looking from Charity and Clem to Kit, as they sat at dinner on their first night home, he put into words what his parents had kept discreetly to themselves.

'I must say you two certainly look blooming, even though Chatty keeps rabbiting on and on about this Luis bloke. Now Kitty-cat here——' He stopped and looked at his sister reprovingly. 'Apart from the shiner, you look skinnier than when you went, even if you are tanned. You look as though you haven't slept for nights, too.'

'Shut up, Pen,' said Clem sharply. 'Kit's a bit tired from the flight, that's all.'

'Come off it,' he scoffed. 'You don't get jet-lag after a flight from Malaga.'

'It was bumpy,' said Chatty firmly.

'I'm a bit older than they are too,' Kit grinned at him, unmoved.

'I bet they ran you ragged!' jeered Penry.

'No, they did not.' Kit's grin altered to a frown.

154

'They were as good as gold and perfectly well behaved; never gave me a moment's anxiety the whole time.'

'It would almost appear to be the other way round,' murmured Mrs Vaughan. 'Have some tart, Kit. Your favourite, blackberry.'

Kit meekly accepted the portion of unwanted tart with its topping of whipped cream, the automatic refusal stifled as she saw the inexorable look in her mother's eye. She ate most of the tart while Dr Vaughan turned the conversation to their accommodation and details of the *Golondrina*, a subject that engrossed everyone, most of all Penry, who was vocally envious about this particular part of the holiday. Charity was only too eager to supply details of the ketch, even more about its joint owners, and the rest of the meal was devoted to details of Luis and his charm, corroborated goodnaturedly by her sisters, who were sincere in their liking for the young Spaniard, which reassured their parents somewhat. The telephone rang a little while later as the girls washed up while their still impeded mother sat and directed operations. Charity's face lit up like a torch.

'Luis!' she exclaimed, and tore out of the room. Seconds later she returned, deflated. 'It's for you, Kit.'

'Who is it?' Kit threw off her apron and hurried off as Charity just shrugged.

Thinking it must be Jon Castle welcoming her home, she made her voice deliberately gay as she picked up the receiver and said hello. She was instantly very still as she heard the unmistakable clipped tones of Reid's voice on the line.

'Hello, Katharine. How are you?'

She swallowed silently and smiled brightly, then wiped the smile off her face again as no one was there to see.

'I'm just fine, thank you. How nice of you to ring. Where are you speaking from?'

'The Florida. Are you really all right?'

'Of course. It was a perfectly uneventful flight, and my father was at Heathrow to meet us; what more could I ask? It's Charity who is in need of sympathy, not me.'

'Katharine!' His voice became rougher, more urgent. 'That's not what I meant, and you know it. I didn't come and see you off today because—well, I didn't want another public dressing down, even if I'm well aware I merit it.'

'Nonsense!' Kit kept her tone deliberately light. 'Nothing of the sort. It was a pleasure meeting you, and all the others. Give my love to Milagrita and wish her well with Juan. I hope your business talks all went smoothly.'

'To hell with all that! Kit, please, I must talk to you. I'll be back in the U.K. by midweek——'

Suddenly Kit could take no more.

'Please Reid. There's nothing to say, really.'

'God, woman, listen to me!'

'Goodbye, Reid.'

She put down the phone and stood looking at it blankly for a moment, then went back to the kitchen.

'You didn't say it was Reid,' she said casually to Charity, who looked uncomfortable.

'He told me not to.'

'Ah, I see.'

Mrs Vaughan looked from one to the other in enquiry.

'I'm glad *you* do, but I certainly don't. Why should this man want to remain anonymous?'

Kit was saved from reply by the shrilling of the phone once more, and Charity flew off to answer it again, her face alight with hope, but seconds later she called Kit before tearing upstairs in obvious disappointment.

'Go and answer it for me, Clem,' she said calmly, putting away dishes efficiently. 'If it's Reid again would you say I'm out, in the bath, gone jogging—anything you like.'

Clem gave a despairing look at her mother, who waved her off quickly to do as Kit asked.

'You disapprove, Mother?' Kit looked at her parent warily.

'Yes. Do your own dirty work in future,' said Mrs Vaughan surprisingly. 'If you don't want to speak to the man that's your own business entirely. I disapprove of expecting other people to tell him so for you, however. Now shall we have coffee in the sitting-room? I shall expect you to admire my amazing dexterity with these crutches by the way; or should the word really *be* dexterity when applied to feet?'

'Don't you start on semantics, too, Mother.' Kit's eyes were over-bright as she picked up the coffee tray and followed Mrs Vaughan's laudably nimble progress across the hall past the now mercifully silent telephone.

The instrument was never silent for long in the Vaughan household, however, both due to the exigencies of Dr Vaughan's profession, and, in the week before the twins departed for art school, to the calls Luis made nightly from Spain, which eventually had to be strictly rationed, as Dr Vaughan objected when the line was occupied for too long at a time. It was settled that Luis would come to visit when Charity came home to Llanhowell for the Christmas holiday break, and only this fact made it bearable for her to set off for college in a reasonably cheerful frame of mind. The house settled down to near normality after the twins' departure. Mrs Vaughan's plaster was eventually removed, Kit was back in her dispensary at the practice and Penry knuckled down to preparations for his fourth-term Oxbridge entrance exam.

Life was back to its usual busy routine. Almost. Mrs Vaughan watched Kit unobtrusively, but with increasing anxiety. There was nothing concrete to account for her disquiet, but some indefinable something in her eldest daughter's manner troubled her deeply. As the days went by Kit ate little and talked more than usual, her animation so unforced that Dr Vaughan and Penry were unaware of any change. Mrs Vaughan made no comment on lack of appetite and listened, as she always did, to Kit's lighthearted accounts of daily incidents that happened in the practice, all of them highly amusing. Life was apparently one long giggle. Only once had Mrs Vaughan delicately enquired if Kit would like to talk about the mysterious Mr Livesey, whose telephone calls had not been repeated since her first day home. Kit had opened her sleepy blue eyes and turned a blank gaze on her mother, assuring her there was little to tell; just one or two meetings after the Granada incident, and that was absolutely all there was to it, honestly.

Mrs Vaughan had made no comment and kept her own counsel for a while, eventually telling her husband their daughter had protested a shade too much. Which was no more than the unvarnished truth, as Kit could have confirmed. During the first days in work she had to fight to concentrate on the demands of her job. Only the fact that the public's well-being, and even safety, relied on her accuracy made her close her mind to the events in Spain. Evenings were a different matter. Jon Castle was more often than not available with demands on her time, and Kit made herself accept his invitations to a meal or the cinema, occasionally to a club where he was a member, to dance and meet friends. She had danced only once with Reid, thought Kit sadly one night. She was moving round a small dance floor with Jon to a rare slow number, and forced the thought away to concentrate guiltily on her companion, to such effect that he misunderstood entirely, becoming distressingly amorous on the way home, with the result that Kit left him angry and truculent, and stormed into the house with colour high.

Surprisingly her mother was in the sitting room reading, an unusual occurrence when Kit went out. Angharad Vaughan had stopped waiting up for her sensible eldest daughter long since.

'Hello, darling, I'm drinking tea,' she smiled, and waved at the tray alongside her. 'Like some?'

Kit accepted a cup and sat down on the other side of the dying fire, staring moodily into the embers. She glanced curiously across at her mother.

'Insomnia, Mother, or am I too late getting in, or something? Am I about to have my hand slapped?'

'I wouldn't dare; you look far too militant, love.' Mrs Vaughan smiled cheerfully and placed a marker in her book. 'I thought I'd wait to tell you that your Mr Livesey rang tonight.'

Kit's stomach gave an odd, cold contraction, as surprising as it was unpleasant. She had genuinely considered herself immune to any reaction Reid's name might cause.

'Really?' Her attempt to sound unaffected failed miserably. 'I thought he'd received my message, loud and clear. Did you just say I was out?'

'Not exactly. I said I could *truthfully* say you were out.'

'And?'

'He sounds very charming. Apparently he went to Brazil for a while after returning from Spain. I gather his home is there.' Mrs Vaughan was deliberately tantalising, studying her daughter's stony profile. 'The point of his call was that he has some business in Newport, but has decided to put up in Monmouth after your description of the town.'

'How interesting,' said Kit flatly, her stomach now churning. 'You had quite a nice little chat, by the sound of it.'

Her mother ignored the sarcasm and rose to her feet, yawning delicately.

'Yes, we did. He asked could he call to see you tomorrow, so I invited him to lunch.'

Kit sprang to her feet, her eyes hot with accusation.

'You did what? Mother! What on earth possessed you? I don't want to see him—I'll go out——'

'No, Katharine.' Something in Angharad's musical, calm voice halted Kit. 'Mr Livesey wants to see *you*. I've invited him to lunch for just this purpose, so you will oblige me by being present. After tomorrow, of course, you may pursue whatever course you like.'

Kit took a very long, deep breath. She swallowed hard.

'You realise, Mother, that if I were a teenager I would have belted out of the room telling you what to do with your beastly lunch?'

Mrs Vaughan inspected the dead fire, then put out the lights and drew the curtains.

'I find it hard to visualise any daughter of mine behaving in such a barbarous manner.' She smiled at

Kit and kissed her cheek lovingly. 'And the whole point is that you're *not* a teenager. Goodnight, darling.'

Kit followed her mother upstairs with her mind in a turmoil, wondering bitterly what her beloved parent thought she was up to. Just when memories of the ill-fated holiday were beginning to fade, too. Over the past few days there had been times when her mind had been free of Reid for several minutes on end, and hope had glimmered that a breakthrough was imminent. Kit had no delusions about her feelings. It had taken her a long time before experiencing the emotion, but it was none the less instantly recognisable. She was in love for the first time in her life; with a man so self-contained and sure of himself she couldn't bear the prospect of facing him after that unspeakable evening on the *Golondrina*. Even now her thoughts shied away from what had passed between them on the boat, finding it almost more bearable to remember the misery of being violently sick while Reid held her head. One way and another she was amazed that he should want to see her again at all. Up to now their encounters had scarcely been tranquil affairs, and the last time she had been a bit public with her refusal of his company on that final evening. What on earth had brought the man to Wales? She was sure his field was with foreign transactions. Whatever his business was, he was having Sunday lunch at the Vaughan household, so she had no option but to put as brave a face on it as possible.

This sensible decision was made with admirable resolution in the early hours of the morning, but sticking to it next day was a different kettle of fish.

'Who's this bloke, then?' demanded Penry over breakfast.

'I met him in Granada.' Kit munched toast morosely and refused to meet her father's speculative eye.

'What does he do?' Dr Vaughan asked mildly, and passed the Sunday supplement over to his wife.

'Works in a bank,' said Kit briefly, willing them to drop the subject.

'Sounds pretty dull.' Penry disposed of the last of his bacon and eggs and heaved himself to his feet. 'Back upstairs to the grind, I suppose.' He looked down gloomily at his rather disgusting jeans. 'I suppose I'll have to change for lunch if this bank chap is coming; he'll be in his gent's natty suiting, no doubt.'

'Forgive me for mentioning it, but personally I would be much happier if you changed for lunch whether we have a visitor or not.' Mrs Vaughan viewed the offending jeans with distaste. 'You're enough to spoil one's appetite in those.'

'Oh, Mam!' Her large son gave Mrs Vaughan a fond squeeze and went off, calling from the stairs, 'Only clean jeans, mind!'

'Anything would be an improvement,' shouted his father, and returned to his Sunday paper with a sigh, enjoying the only morning of the week with leisure to linger over breakfast and newspaper.

Kit rose to clear the table, clattering plates with rather unnecessary force.

'I don't see why all the fuss,' she said irritably. 'I hardly know the man. He was just someone met casually on holiday. Lord knows why he wants to follow it up.'

'Just because he's in the area, I expect. No doubt he's glad to enliven the quiet of a Welsh winter Sunday in Wales.' Mrs Vaughan chuckled as she followed Kit to the kitchen. 'Pity it isn't Wednesday, my alliteration would have been flawless.'

'And I'd be in work!' Kit dumped the tray on a counter, sniffing. 'The meat smells nice. Beef?'

Her mother nodded.

'Tail end of rump. Luckily I had it it in the freezer; I've been saving it——'

'Mother, this is *not* a special occasion!'

'I was *about* to say,' said Mrs Vaughan with dignity, 'until the parsnips had their first frost, so stop jumping down my throat, girl!'

Kit was contrite and put her arms round her mother, laying her head on the familiar comforting shoulder.

'I'm sorry—I'm a pig. A very edgy pig.'

Mrs Vaughan patted her soothingly.

'Understandable. Now let's get on so that we're not rushing about at the last minute.'

'What time is he coming?'

'Twelve-ish. So first we wash up, then I'll sit and do the vegetables while you tidy the sitting room and lay the dining-table.'

Harmony restored, the two worked together efficiently as always, so that well before the appointed hour everything was ready. Kit had made the rich brown gravy and beaten up the Yorkshire pudding batter, the roast potatoes were crisping gently in the oven and the joint was 'relaxing' in the warming oven accompanied by the other vegetables in covered dishes. Kit went upstairs to change, and dispiritedly put on a butterscotch silk shirt with beige velveteen jeans. She was dissatisfied with the result and added a waistcoat in brown and white houndstooth checks and slotted a brown leather belt through the loops of the jeans to match her glossy high-heeled brown leather boots. She augmented her fading tan with a touch of blusher and carefully applied some grey-brown eyeshadow, thankful that all traces of her black eye had now gone, though she would have been glad of the excuse to wear dark glasses. Her room was at the back of the house, and she was so preoccupied with brushing her hair that she was startled when Penry came rushing in to say Reid had arrived.

'Come on, Kitty-cat. Your bank-manager is here—I like his car!'

Kit gave herself a last look in the mirror and followed her brother out of the room, going slowly down the stairs in his wake. Reid stood in the square hall below chatting easily to her parents, wearing a tweed jacket over camel sweater and Bedford cords, a far cry from Penry's 'natty suiting'. Kit fought a deep desire to bolt for cover as she saw him, but he looked up and caught her eye at the same moment, moving to the foot of the stairs to meet her, oblivious of the large figure of her young brother between them.

'Hello, Katharine.' The smile in the hazel eyes halted Kit and it was left to Penry to stand still, giving his sister time to come to life and descend the rest of the stairs to take Reid's outstretched hand.

'Hello, Reid. This is a surprise; to see you in Wales, I mean.'

'I hope you don't mind.' Reid's voice was even and controlled, as usual, but the look in his eyes was completely the opposite, causing havoc with Kit's pulse.

'No, of course not.' Kit grabbed Penry by the hand. 'This is my brother, Penry. Reid Livesey, Pen. We met in Spain.'

It was a well-known fact that all Penry's rough edges were reserved for his family and closest friends. At the moment he was metamorphosed into an admirable example of the best of British education, and was chatting to Reid, with an ease that brought well-concealed approval from his parents and sister as Dr Vaughan directed their visitor to a chair near the brightly burning fire in the sitting-room and offered him whatever he fancied. Reid asked for a small quantity of neat whisky with an apologetic smile.

'After a spell in Spain, followed by a visit to my family in Brazil, in Rio Grande do Sul, I'm having a problem in getting to grips with the British climate again.'

'I don't even use the climate as an excuse.' Dr Vaughan shot a twinkling look at his wife. 'Never been a sherry or gin and tonic man myself.'

'A walking exception to the rule about mixing grape and grain.' Mrs Vaughan smiled ruefully at Reid.

'Moderation is the secret, *cariad*.' Her husband patted her hand, then turned to their guest. 'When did you drive down, Mr Livesey?'

'Yesterday afternoon.' Reid turned to look at Kit, who sat in the armchair opposite with Penry perched on the arm. 'Too late to see your historic Monmouth by daylight, I'm afraid. I had a quick look round this morning—fascinating town.'

Kit smiled faintly, but remained silent, and Mrs Vaughan broke in hastily.

'Do you know much of Britain well?'

'Hardly anything at all. I rarely get the opportunity

to travel outside London apart from trips abroad.'

'Funny old life,' mused Dr Vaughan. 'I don't know that I'd enjoy all that globe-trotting.'

'Kit mentioned a ketch,' put in Penry wistfully. Immediately the conversation became an animated maritime affair of question and answer between the three men on boats and sailing, while Mrs Vaughan left the room to check on the lunch, followed quickly by Kit. She joined her mother in somewhat abstracted mood. Mrs Vaughan was busily occupied with transferring roast potatoes from one oven to the other and inserting the Yorkshire puddings to cook. She straightened, cheeks flushed, to look quizzically at her daughter.

'I can't think why you were so against his coming here, love. He's charming.'

Without blurting out the whole sorry story Kit felt there was little she could say, and shrugged carelessly.

'I had a little fracas with Jon, and I suppose it left me feeling witch-like last night. Put it down to my natural cussedness.'

'Of which you don't have a great deal.' Mrs Vaughan waved her daughter away. 'Nothing to do here for the minute. Go and see if your father is keeping our guest's glass topped up, then direct him out here to open the wine. I'm useless with a corkscrew.'

When Kit returned to the sitting room Reid rose to his feet and she waved him to his seat again before passing on her mother's request to Dr Vaughan. He went off promptly to do his wife's bidding and almost at once the phone rang. Penry sprang to his feet to answer it, closing the door behind him as he left. There was silence in the room while Kit sat down and looked into the fire, aware that Reid was watching her.

'Your eye is better.' Reid spoke softly.

She nodded, keeping her eyes on the flames.

'It faded quite quickly. I was able to get back to my job a week after returning home.'

'And you're completely well? No ill effects after the concussion?'

Kit shifted uncomfortably in her chair, wishing the others would come back.

'None at all. I'm normally a very healthy person, hard though it may be to believe.'

'You've lost weight.' His voice was husky as he leaned forward in his chair.

'Not all that much.'

'Katharine!' The urgent note in his voice made her look up sharply. 'That's better. Your hair is beautiful, but I'd rather look at your face than the top of your head.'

Having looked up Kit found herself unable to look away.

'Why wouldn't you speak to me on the phone?' he went on quietly.

'I'm sorry, that was childish. Put it down to the after-effects of concussion.' Kit smiled hesitantly, and an answering smile immediately lit Reid's face. 'You still have your tan—mine is fading rapidly.'

'I went off to Rio Grande do Sul almost immediately, and I persuaded my brother to take a little time off to do some sailing with me in Porto Alegre, so I'm weatherbeaten.' Reid leaned nearer, his face suddenly tense. 'Katharine, I must talk to you. . . .'

The door opened and Penry sauntered in to announce that lunch was ready.

'That was the demon duo on the phone, Kit. They wouldn't let me call you once they knew you had a visitor.' He grinned broadly at Reid. 'They both sent *you* their love, by the way.'

Reid grinned back.

'I'm very pleased to hear it—charming girls, your sisters!'

'Oh, Kitty-cat here is all right.' Penry put out a hand and pulled Kit to her feet. 'But the other two are a bit wearing on the old nerves, not to mention their nasty leanings towards petty larceny when it comes to certain of my clothes.'

Reid laughed delightedly as they moved towards the door.

'If it's any consolation they certainly looked spectacular in whatever it was they—er—borrowed.'

Penry screwed up his face in disgust as he politely

ushered Kit and Reid ahead of him into the dining room.

The meal passed very pleasantly, with some educated questions from Reid on Dr Vaughan's practice, followed by some information on the Brazilian fazenda that was his own home, where the huge acreage in Rio Grande do Sul ran cattle and sheep, as well as various crops, including tobacco.

After Reid had consumed second helpings of the main course, followed by blackcurrant cobbler, Mrs Vaughan was obviously pleased at his extravagant but obviously sincere praise of her cooking.

'The best I've eaten in this country,' he assured her. 'Though I'm afraid my experience is limited to restaurants rather than private houses.'

'Do you do your own cooking?' Kit asked; the first question she'd volunteered since Reid's arrival.

'I live in a service flat—the only answer for a lonely bachelor in London.' Smiling at her briefly, he turned to Mrs Vaughan again. 'At the risk of boring you I must reiterate my compliments on the food.'

'I'm fortunate, Mr Livesey. Kit always helps with part of it, and even Penry has been known to wield a tea-towel under duress, especially during my recent spell in plaster.'

'Which parts did you contribute today, Katharine?' asked Reid.

'At a guess I'd say the gravy, the Yorkshire pudding and the dessert,' hazarded Dr Vaughan, before Kit could speak. 'Am I right?'

It was hard to recognise the man so much at ease with her family as her unwilling rescuer in Granada. Kit rose to clear away, smiling faintly.

'Dead right, Dad. Up to scratch, I trust?'

'A fraction more sugar in the blackcurrants; your mother makes it sweeter!'

'Be careful, or she won't make it again,' advised Mrs Vaughan. 'Now come into the other room to enjoy our coffee by the fire.'

The cloudy, overcast morning had given way to a crisply bright afternoon, and Reid looked from Dr

Vaughan to his wife after drinking two cups of coffee.

'Would you mind if I took Katharine for a drive? Perhaps she would be kind enough to show me the out-of-the-way places tourists never find.'

To Kit's embarrassment his suggestion met with rather obvious approval from at least three of the Vaughans, as even Penry was patently well disposed towards Reid.

'Well, Katharine?' Reid looked directly at her. 'Will you come?'

She hesitated a little, then nodded and stood up.

'We'd better start off straight away, then, before the light fades.'

Kit went upstairs to fetch her sheepskin jacket while Reid made his farewells to her parents and repeated his thanks for the meal. Only pausing to snatch up the bag that matched her boots, she ran down to find everyone outside admiring Reid's BMW, shining in the afternoon sun. Reid himself was more interested in the haphazard charm of the garden, picturesque despite its late autumn untidiness. He opened the door of the car as Kit appeared, and settled her in before getting behind the wheel, guiding the car slowly down the leaf-strewn drive, and out into the deserted Sunday quiet of the road.

Kit gave a few directions, and they set off to explore the beautiful scenery of the area around Monmouth, meandering along narrow minor back roads away from the main bypass.

'Your family were very kind to a stranger,' remarked Reid. 'Their hospitality is impressive. I was hesitant to take your mother up on her invitation last night, but she was very insistent, and I accepted with some misgivings. I was fairly sure you'd be angry.'

'I was,' said Kit frankly. 'When I came home I blew my top.'

'Where had you been?' he asked casually, peering at road signs with long, unfamiliar Welsh names on them.

'To a country club to dine and dance with one of the doctors who works with my father.' Kit's lips compressed as she thought of Jon's behaviour.

Reid glanced at her briefly.

'It seems you didn't enjoy your evening too much; and then you got home to find I was coming to lunch today. Or didn't you learn that until this morning?'

'Mother considered the news of sufficient interest to stay up until I arrived home—which wasn't so very late, really.'

'And were you angry?'

Kit sighed.

'My first impulse was to go out for the day, but my mother soon scotched that idea, in no uncertain terms. She has a telling way of putting one in one's place on occasion.'

'Do you dislike me so much, then, Katharine?' Reid kept his eyes steadily on the road, his face set.

'No, it wasn't that. I was embarrassed, that's all, and —well, I thought I would never meet you again. I wasn't too enchanted at the thought of coming face to face with you again after—well, after that night.'

'Katharine, I would give a lot to undo some of that night,' he said, sighing, 'but——'

'Take the second left along here,' Kit interrupted.

Reid did as she said, then looked sideways at her, smiling wryly.

'This just isn't on. Is there somewhere we can park and just talk uninterrupted for a while?'

Kit did her best to conceal her suddenly accelerated pulse-rate, and nodded meekly.

'Yes. Just along here there's a very small layby with a view of the river. There it is.'

Never very busy, the narrow road was deserted on this late autumn afternoon, despite the weak sunshine, and they had the layby to themselves. Reid unclipped his seatbelt and turned to look at Kit. There was a silence for a while; Kit looking steadfastly ahead through the windscreen, and Reid with his eyes unwavering on her profile.

'Is everything all right with you, Kit?' he asked eventually, his voice stern, making her start slightly.

She nodded, not looking at him.

'Yes. I'm completely over my labyrynthitis, the

concussion, my eye is merely blue, instead of various other colours. In fact you could say I'm as normal as whatever normal is.'

He frowned and put out a hand, gently bringing her face round so that he could look deep into her eyes, which flickered before the expression in his.

'I think you know what I'm asking. In the middle of all the other sensations I experienced that night I was shattered to find that—well, that——'

'You were proceeding where no man had gone before?' she suggested, brutally flippant to conceal her agitation.

A dull red crept under the dark tan of Reid's face, and his thick brows came together in a straight line.

'Don't try to cheapen what happened, Katharine. You can't possibly make me feel any lower than I do already. I'm not exactly proud of my behaviour, but, at the risk of making excuses, you must know that by the time I discovered the truth it was impossible to do anything about it.' He sighed raggedly. 'After all, you must admit you could have said something sooner.'

'I do admit it, freely. I'm not blaming you, only myself.' Kit was deliberately matter-of-fact, trying to disregard the electricity that fairly crackled between them. 'So you see, you came a long way for absolutely nothing. I don't hold you responsible for anything.'

He winced, his mouth tightening, a white line round his lips as he looked away to stare at the scene in front of them. Miserably Kit stared in the same direction, the charm of the scene utterly lost on them both as the fading light filtered through bare branches over the fields that gave on to the River Monnow, smoke rising in the distance from a small hillside farmhouse.

She started violently when Reid finally said harshly,

'This is sheer stupidity. I'm skating all round the subject when all the time both you and I know damn well the crux of the matter.' He leaned over her urgently, and Kit shrank back in her seat, trying to escape the familiar yellow light in the searching eyes. 'Look at me, for God's sake! I know how old you are, and if—well, if by some miracle I was the first to—the first, I haven't been able to rid myself of the fear that a child is not out of the question.'

'Fear?' Kit eyed him with dislike, moving ostentatiously away. 'You have nothing at all to fear, I can assure you.'

Reid ran his hand distractedly over this thick hair, subsiding back to look blindly through the windscreen again.

'You mean you aren't pregnant?' he said baldly.

Kit flushed, painful hot colour beating along her cheekbones.

'Will you take me home, please?' Her face was rigid with distaste.

'My God, no, I won't! At least, not until we get things straight.' Reid was practically shouting, and he made a visible effort to control himself. He put out a hand and grasped her cold, unresponsive fingers.

'Katharine, please. I realise this is a painful subject to discuss, but I must know. Are you pregnant?'

There was a short silence, then Kit gasped suddenly as his fingers crushed hers painfully as though he meant to shock an answer out of her.

'All right, Katharine,' he said huskily. 'You would have said "no" only too quickly if you weren't, so I take it from your silence that it's possible you are.'

Kit sighed and closed her eyes, leaning her head back against the car-rest.

'I must be honest and say I'm not sure yet.' She turned miserable blue eyes on his tense face. 'Shall we say I've had three weeks to wonder about it, and worry.'

Reid's eyes closed momentarily, then opened to smile down at her reassuringly.

'No worrying from now on. There's an obvious solution, surely.'

Kit's face went blank, her whole body rigid with tension as she looked fixedly up into his face.

'Just what is it you have in mind?' she asked evenly.

With a curiously casual tone in his voice Reid said jauntily:

'I think we should go back to your parents and tell them we're going to be married.'

Kit's eyes opened wide in sheer disbelief.

'Are you joking?'

'No,' he said, 'practical. This way no one will ever suspect we're marrying for anything other than the normal reason.'

The corners of Kit's mouth turned down.

'I thought this *was* the normal reason these days,' she said acidly. 'Otherwise people just sort of move in with each other, don't they?'

'I'm not concerned with other people. I'm concerned about you—and about your family,' Reid slid an arm round her shoulders, pulling her rigid body towards him. 'Neither of us is a child. I'm not in the least averse to marrying you, Katharine. It's high time I settled down, according to my family, and I feel certain you and I could make a success of life together.'

Kit laughed; a lost, humourless little sound.

'There you go again! Any minute you'll be discussing viability and feasibility as though marriage were some business proposition. . . .'

'Ah, but you left out compatibility,' he said softly, and quickly kissed her unsuspecting mouth, holding her closely against his chest. Kit held herself stiffly for a few moments while his mouth coaxed hers, her body unyielding despite the pressure of the hard arm that held her captive. Gradually she relaxed, leaning against him, aware of the slight roughness of his tweed jacket against her cheek, a feeling of rightness at being where she was. With a sigh she opened her mouth to the increasing insistence of his lips and abruptly all the peace and languor vanished. Reid's hands were no longer gentle as he pressed her harder against him and kissed her with an urgency that began to produce feelings Kit recognised with alarm.

'No!' she gasped, pushing herself upright and twisting her head away.

'Kit!' Reid moved after her, his hands hard on her shoulders. 'Look at me!'

She shook her head, eyes shut, blindly trying to calm the tumult inside her, struggling frantically as his mouth crushed down on hers again. One hand found the handle of the car door and pressed, the sudden stream of cold air halting Reid's onslaught.

'For God's sake,' he panted, leaning across her to pull the door shut. 'You'll fall out!'

Kit glared at him, her breath coming in jerky gasps.

'At least it stopped you slavering over me!'

Even as the words left her mouth she would have given the world to unsay them. Reid became still, his breathing slowing gradually as he sat in brooding silence.

'That, I think you might say, would appear to be that,' he said bitterly. 'Far be it from me to—er—slaver over anyone.'

'I'm sorry. It was an unfortunate word to choose,' said Kit stiffly. 'I didn't mean to be quite so offensive.'

Gingerly Reid took her hand in his, looking at her in wry enquiry.

'What words do you use when actually *intending* to be offensive?'

She smiled in spite of herself.

'I'm sorry.'

'That's better, Miss Vaughan. Now can we return to the matter in hand?' His sudden grin disarmed her, quite different from the usual guarded smile that Kit found so daunting. She relaxed back in the comfortable seat, prepared for reasonable discussion.

'You don't have to marry me, you know,' she began looking at him squarely. 'It's not absolutely certain yet, and even if—well, the very worst happens, you don't have to carry your Don Quixote role that far. Besides, I can't make myself believe there's really need for concern—there could be other reasons. . . .' She flushed, but went on doggedly. 'After all, I was ill before the holiday, then I had the fright in Granada, and the concussion on the ketch. Any of those things could be the reason for my system to have gone a bit haywire.'

'Katharine,' he said slowly, the look in his eyes tender as he saw her embarrassment, 'would you find it so very hard to believe that I might just want to marry you anyway?'

She looked startled, her eyes wide and questioning on his.

'Yes, I'm afraid I would. We hardly know each other. . . .'

'Long enough, at our respective ages, surely?' Something in the way he was looking at her made Kit tremble, and she looked determinedly through the window into the deepening dusk.

'I don't believe in love at first sight; that's strictly for fiction.'

'Who said anything about love?' The indulgent note in his voice stung Kit unbearably. 'You are an intelligent, attractive, mature woman that any man would be happy to have as his partner. Once I can persuade you to stop fighting me I think you'll admit we're physically compatible, and your lack of promiscuity is proven beyond all doubt. What more could I ask?'

Kit was unconvinced.

'And if all this worry and concern proves to be unnecessary—what then? Do these virtues of mine still make the thought of marriage attractive, or will the removal of necessity come down too heavily on the side of bachelorhood and feedom?'

'I thought I was making that crystal clear by suggesting marriage immediately,' Reid said impatiently, 'instead of waiting until you're sure, and frankly, from what you say, it seems a fairly cast-iron certainty to me.'

Kit sat looking down at the toes of her boots for some considerable time, Reid sitting back in his seat to leave her undisturbed in her thinking. Eventually she looked up at his profile, hardly discernible now in the twilight.

'All right then,' she said quietly. 'I'll take you up on your offer.'

Even in the dim light it was obvious Reid was startled.

'Just like that?'

'Well, what else would you like me to say? That I'm sensible of the honour you do me, and take great pleasure in bestowing my hand in marriage? How's that?'

He eyed her, perplexed, making no move to kiss her in acknowledgment.

'No kiss for your betrothed?' asked Kit caustically.

Reid rubbed his chin ruefully.

'Somehow it would seem more appropriate to be signing a contract, or some sort of agreement, with witnesses, etc.'

Kit smiled at him kindly.

'We shan't need those until the register office, when we tie the knot. You're a bit confused.'

'I agree. Except that I dislike the register office bit. We passed a very picturesque village church not far from your home this afternoon. I feel sure your parents would like us to be married there.'

Kit's flippancy left her instantly.

'But you don't really *mean* all this, Reid? Honestly, there's probably no need——'

'I think it's time I took you home,' he cut in, and started the engine, looking over his shoulder as he reversed the car. 'Do you think your mother will offer me tea?'

'A pity Dad snatched her first,' said Kit with sarcasm. 'You could have married her instead!'

A brief gleam of white teeth was his only response, and he kept firmly to neutral topics on the journey back to Llanhowell. The front door flew open as Reid turned the car in to the Vaughans' driveway, revealing Penry's silhouette against the welcoming light within.

'They're back, Mam,' he shouted over his shoulder, then grinned in welcome as Kit and Reid got out of the car. 'Thought you'd never come; Mam wouldn't start tea until you did.'

Giving Kit a gleaming look of triumph, Reid followed her into the house, to be greeted by Mrs Vaughan and shooed through to the sitting room where a laden tea-trolley waited and a roaring fire cast out warmth and light to dispel any late autumnal chill. Dr Vaughan had obviously been enjoying a nap and smiled sleepily as Reid sat down next to Kit on the big chintz-covered settee.

'Had a pleasant little trip?'

'Very enjoyable,' said Reid, 'some lovely scenery in this part of the world.'

'Can't have seen much of it for the past hour,' observed Penry, with a wicked grin. 'It's dark.'

His mother turned a cold, quelling blue eye on him and pressed her guest to hot buttered scones, Welsh cakes and bara brith, all of which he tucked into with an enthusiasm which made up for Kit's lack of appetite.

When Reid had eaten a satisfactory amount by even Penry's standards, he set his tea cup down on the small table beside him and said quite casually to Dr Vaughan,

'I believe I should be asking your permission, sir, but I sincerely hope neither you nor Mrs Vaughan have any objection to the fact that I wish to marry Katharine.'

In the ensuing excitement there was little need for Kit to do anything but smile, which was just as well, as she was lost for words. She gazed at Reid as her father and Penry wrung his hand, and her mother kissed his cheek, finally getting to her feet to stand obediently within the circle of his arm to receive her share of kisses and congratulations. Reid looked down at her with such warmth in his eyes that her cheeks flamed, as she well knew how closely her mother was viewing the proceedings.

'You won't be stealing her off too quickly, I hope,' said Dr Vaughan later on when the first flurry of excitement had died down.

'It all depends on what you mean by "soon".' Reid's possessive arm tightened round Kit as she tensed, waiting for his answer. 'How about a month from yesterday? Will that give us time to call the banns?'

CHAPTER NINE

KIT felt as though a juggernaut had run over her by the time Reid finally left that night, confessing quite blatantly that his business in Newport had been completely fictitious. This merely added to his lustre as far as the rest of the Vaughans were concerned, all three obviously impressed by his coming to Monmouth in sole pursuit of Kit. He was returning to London at the crack of dawn next day, and made his farewells to Kit in private later that night, the others having tactfully departed to bed beforehand.

'You rather jumped the gun,' remarked Kit.

'Left to you I had the feeling the whole thing would have been swept under the carpet like so much dust.' Reid pulled her against him and she lay with her head on his chest, listening to the steady, reassuring beat of his heart as she stared rather dazedly into the fire, trying to come to terms with the new development in her life.

'Did you really mean it—about marrying in a month's time?' she asked doubtfully.

Reid's arms tightened.

'If I could make it sooner I would, but a special licence might smack of indecent haste, so we'll stick to the banns and I'll come down to Monmouth each weekend.'

'You don't have to put up at a hotel, you can stay here.' Kit twisted round to look up at him.

He shook his head, smiling wryly as he kissed the tip of her nose.

'No. I shall defer sleeping under the same roof until we're married. I would find it difficult knowing you were only a few feet away in another room.'

Kit lay looking up at him wonderingly.

'You know, one of the reasons why you annoyed me was that you always look so much in control; of yourself and everyone else.'

'I used to kid myself I was. Then I found you wavering all over the car park at the Alhambra, and life altered dramatically.' The teasing light in his eyes changed as they looked down into hers. 'Are you sorry?'

'No.' The droop in Kit's eyelids and on her full mouth conveyed a message she was unaware of transmitting.

'Katharine——' Involuntarily Reid kissed her yielding mouth, her sudden lack of opposition going to his head. He bent over her, his lips questing and caressing, his fingers sliding beneath the silk of her shirt. 'This is where you're supposed to fight me,' he said hoarsely, burying his face in her hair.

'Why?' Kit turned up her mouth to his with such spontaneity he was defeated, lost to everything but the feel of the slender body in his arms until the chiming of the clock in the hall pierced through the cocoon of desire that enveloped them both.

Reid rose unwillingly to his feet, breathing deeply, and pulled Kit up with him. He fastened her shirt with unsteady fingers and smiled crookedly into her flushed face, smoothing back the dark, tangled hair.

'Now you see why I'll stick to a hotel!' He kissed her again briefly, then put her gently but firmly away from him. 'I must go. See me to the door.'

'When are you coming again?' Kit leaned against the lintel of the open front door, still only half believing what had happened.

'Friday evening if possible, Saturday morning if not. I'll ring you. Goodnight, sweet Kate, be good until next weekend.' Reid kissed her again, his hands leaving her with reluctance.

'And how do you want me to behave next weekend?' Kit smiled wickedly, suddenly self-assured, enjoying the scowl he turned on her.

'Make it easy for me to go, Katharine,' he said softly, utterly serious.

She put out a hand shyly and touched his cheek.

'Goodnight, Reid.' She shut the door quietly, making her way slowly to bed, her mind in a whirl. But rather a nice whirl, she thought, a secretive little smile curling up the corners of her mouth. She opened her bedroom door to find Mrs Vaughan lying comfortably on the bed, propped up against the pillows with a magazine across her knees.

'That's rather a triumphant little smile,' said Mrs Vaughan dispassionately, 'which, all things considered, is hardly surprising.'

'You should be in bed,' said Kit reprovingly, and sat on the dressing table stool. 'Did you like Reid?'

'Yes, darling, of course I did.' Her mother shook an admonishing finger at her. 'You've really been rather devious, haven't you—all that fuss last night when you knew he was coming! You gave the impression you actively disliked him.'

'We had a bit of a disagreement in Spain,' said Kit evasively, 'and he came down here to patch things up.'

'Patch things up!' Mrs Vaughan chuckled. 'Bit of an understatement, love, wouldn't you say?'

'Reid insisted on getting married as soon as possible. Do you mind?'

'I would have liked a bit more notice, naturally, but you're both adults, and by the sound of it he's well able to support you.'

'As if that mattered!' snorted Kit.

'How many guests do you want?' asked her mother, changing the subject.

Kit was taken aback.

'I've no idea. We didn't discuss that. I don't suppose his parents will come all that way, though I don't know.' She looked up in appeal. 'Mother, I don't want a big fuss, no white satin and veil and all that, just a few relatives and friends.'

Mrs Vaughan got up, yawning. She kissed Kit lovingly, giving her a hug.

'You have whatever you like, darling, we'll sort it out tomorrow. Now go to sleep, relax. Put it out of your mind for the time being, and get rid of those blue marks under your eyes.' She turned in the doorway. 'We must let Charity and Clem know as soon as we can—they'll be ecstatic. I gather they felt you were extremely hard on Reid in Spain, for some reason. Goodnight, Katharine.'

Kit literally danced through her work for the next few days, her father's patients generally of the opinion that her smile did them just as much good as the medicine she put up for them. Reid rang up every evening, only curtailing his conversation on the nights Dr Vaughan was on call. He agreed readily with Kit's idea of a small, quiet wedding, suggesting a honeymoon trip to Brazil to meet his parents and save them the long trip to the wedding. His father and mother were apparently delighted at Reid's news, and sent loving messages to Kit, while Reid's brother would be coming to the wedding in the dual role of family representative and best man.

As the numbers were small Mrs Vaughan decided to have the wedding buffet at home, with the help of a local firm of caterers, the church was reserved for the required day and she watched her daughter with a glad thankfulness, rejoicing for her in her sudden happiness. It proved to be not only sudden but fleeting.

Towards the end of the week the glow was gone, quenched, as though the lamp of Kit's joy had been switched off. All enquiries about her health met with negative replies. She was fine, no vertigo, no nausea, no influenza, not even beri-beri or psittacosis, she said crossly, after one enquiry too many. Angharad Vaughan kept her counsel, and worried. The nightly phone calls from Reid continued, and these, at least, were obviously satisfactory, if Kit's heightened colour and temporary rise in spirits were anything to go by. But the improvement was transient, and Kit soon became abstracted and quiet again. When this was pointed out to Dr Vaughan he watched his daughter unobtrusively and became as concerned as his wife.

As she and Kit were preparing dinner together one evening Mrs Vaughan could contain herself no longer.

'Not getting cold feet at this stage, darling, are you?' She strove to keep her tone light. 'That's supposed to attack you just before the wedding day.'

Kit shook her head and went on stirring gravy.

'No, of course not. I think that wretched virus left my personality a bit out of Kilter, that's all. I seem to be more up and down than I used to, with the accent on "down".'

'Never mind, I expect the swing will be to "up" by the weekend. When's Reid coming?'

'Friday, about eight, he says.' Kit reached for the salt, her back to her mother.

'Your father and I won't be here; it's Penry's school play. *Henry VI Part One*—or is it *Part Two*? It won't matter either way, Henry isn't precisely a Shakespeare fan, I'm afraid.'

'Penry's not performing, surely?' Kit actually smiled at the prospect.

'No. He's one of the stage crew, but we have to put in an appearance.'

The rest of the week brought no improvement. Kit took herself off to work and immersed herself in her job to such an extent that she was fatigued and lacklustre when she got home each night. On the Friday Mrs Vaughan got ready early for her evening at Penry's school, leaving the main bathroom free for Kit.

'Your father can have a shower if there's time. Penry's staying in school, so the field's clear for a good wallow,' she instructed.

Kit smiled and kissed her.

'Thanks, Mother. Did you make anything for our dinner, or shall I do something?'

'You didn't say, darling, and I thought you might be tired, especially on a Friday, so I half prepared it. Two large vol-au-vents to heat up in the oven, and there's a pan on top of the stove with some prawn filling to warm with care—add a little more cream and brandy as you go—frozen petits pois and ratatouille to go with it and a raspberry pavlova for dessert.'

'You're a wizard!' Kit smiled in appreciation, taking in her mother's appearance with an approving eye. 'Your hair looks gorgeous, the picture of an elegant school mother.' She glanced at her watch. 'Dad said he'll be home at half-past six and he's starving—is he having vol-au-vent?'

'Naturally, can't show favouritism to newcomers. Here's a glass of sherry. Go and drink it slowly in the bath with a book; I've been to the library.' Mrs Vaughan watched her daughter's slow ascent upstairs anxiously, then returned to the kitchen as her husband's car drew up on the gravel drive outside.

Kit poured bath oil into deep hot water, and tied up her hair on top of her head, letting herself down into the foam with a sigh. She took her sherry and the latest Evelyn Anthony from the cork-topped stool alongside the bath and concentrated on the novel's intricate plot fiercely, the story gripping her in spite of herself, and she was quite surprised when her mother called goodbye.

'Have a good time!' shouted Kit, and sat up to look at her watch. Just gone seven, Reid could be here in an hour. She hesitated, undecided whether to linger a few minutes more in the bath, but her desire to read had gone, and she began to lather herself all over before patting herself dry and smoothing fragrant lotion into skin which was still brown from the Spanish sun. Without much interest she went back to her own room to look through her clothes, eventually putting on a hyacinth blue silk shirt and swirling mid-calf skirt in fine pale grey tweed, its waistband emphasised by a belt of gleaming black cobra-skin and silver links. Like an automaton she carefully drew on gossamer-fine powder grey stockings and grey kid sandals with fragile heels, threaded silver hoops through her earlobes, wound a silver chain several times round one slim wrist and began to make up her face. This evening all her movements seemed precise and methodical, the hand holding her mascara brush as steady as a rock. Just as though someone had wound me up with a key, thought Kit starting slightly as the phone rang. She ran to her parents' bedroom and picked up the extension, her heart thumping as Reid said,

'Hello. Katharine?'

'Yes—yes, Reid.' He wasn't coming. Her mouth dried.

'I'm in Newport, filling up the car. I don't know how

long it takes from here to your place, but that's how long I'll be.' He paused. 'Are you there, Katharine?'

Weak with relief, she said huskily.

'Yes, of course. I'll have dinner ready.'

'See you soon.'

Kit flew down the stairs, switched on the oven, put water to heat for the peas, started heating the prawn mixture with care, as instructed, noting with a smile of gratitude for her mother that the trolley was laid with everything necessary, including wineglasses.

By the time the doorbell rang the vegetables were cooked, the pastry cases were warming through in the oven, and Kit was in a high state of nerves. She ran to open the front door, smiling in welcome as Reid came into the warm hall with a rush, throwing off his fur-lined jacket and catching her in a rib-cracking hug, kissing her until she was breathless.

His eyes glittered as he muttered 'Sorry', and rubbed noses with her. 'I should have said "hello" first. Hello Katharine!'

'Hello, Reid.' Kit took him by the hand and led him to the kitchen, waving him to a chair. 'Sit and talk to me—I'm putting the dinner together; Mother and Dad are at Penry's school play.'

'Is Penry at Penry's school play too?' Reid looked at her in speculation.

'Of course, he's one of the stage crew. They need someone his size to heave scenery about.' Kit's colour heightened as Reid rose to his feet very deliberately and stalked towards her in disturbingly predatory manner. 'Now stop it—you'll ruin Mother's vol-au-vents—mind the spoon, you'll get sauce on your jacket. . . .'

All further protests were lost as he grabbed her, spoon and all, and kissed her hungrily.

'Never mind the vol-au-vents,' he murmured, and nibbled at her lips, moving over to her ears. 'You're just as edible, and twice as delicious—mmm!'

Kit was laughing helplessly in spite of herself at her first experience of Reid in playful mood.

'Stop it at once,' she said primly, trying vainly to

stifle her giggles as his hands tickled her waist and he blew on the side of her neck. 'Now look——'

'I am looking,' he said meekly, and gazed down into her eyes so soulfully she was hardly able to shove him away for laughing.

'Have a drink, for heaven's sake,' she implored, 'while I put this meal on the trolley and we can laze in front of the sitting-room fire and picnic.'

Reid gave a long, contented sigh, and stayed where he was.

'I don't need a drink. Just let me watch and revel in unaccustomed domesticity, please.'

Kit looked at him sharply, but realised he was completely sincere.

'Will you open the wine, then, you'll find some in the fridge.'

He obeyed promptly and Kit watched him with surreptitious pleasure as she carefully filled the pastry cases with their mouthwatering prawn mixture. Everything about him pleased her fastidious eye, from the way his hair grew thick and close to his head, just reaching the collar of his cream shantung shirt, to the elegant brown suit and quiet tie in muted beige silk. He looked up to see her watching him.

'What's the matter?'

'I was thinking how elegant you looked.' Pink-cheeked, she smiled uncertainly as he moved instinctively towards her then stopped, frowning.

'Katharine, if you want me to remain docile and biddable it would be better not to make remarks like that. May I take my jacket off?'

'Yes, you may take your jacket off, but I must be honest and say that docile and biddable are not words I associate with you!' She stuck her tongue out, then backed away as she saw the look on his face. 'Will you wheel the trolley in for me?'

'When you smile at me like that I'll do anything on earth for you.' Reid was deadly serious for a moment, then he smiled cheerfully. 'Come on then, let's go and have your picnic.'

They sat on the floor in the sitting room, legs

outstretched and backs to the settee while they ate the tempting meal with varying degrees of appetite, Reid hugely and Kit moderately. While he ate Reid told Kit how pleased his parents had been when he rang to tell them the news. They were impatient to meet their son's bride, and were sending all sorts of gifts with Rico when he flew over for the wedding. Juan and Milagrita had been informed, and, of course, Luis and Carlos, and they were all delighted and happy to come to the wedding. Eventually Reid broke off as Kit's silence became noticeable.

'What is it, Katharine?' Reid examined her face with concern as she gathered up the plates and put them on the trolley.

'I'll take this out and bring in the coffee,' she said, summoning up a bright smile. 'Shan't be a moment.'

When Kit came back with the coffee tray Reid was standing in front of the fireplace, arms folded, his brows in a straight line, all levity vanished.

'Changed your mind?' he asked quietly.

'Black or white?' said Kit desperately.

'To hell with the coffee!' Reid seized her wrist and brought her up hard against him, the other hand turning up her face to his. 'Well, Katharine? Answer me.'

Kit swallowed dryly.

'It—it isn't necessary any more,' she blurted.

'What isn't necessary?' His frown grew blacker.

'Getting married.' Miserably Kit passed the tip of her tongue around her dry lips. 'All those other reasons I mentioned in the car last Sunday—apparently I was right. One of them, or all of them, was responsible for the hiccup in my usual procedure, not—well, not what I suspected. So you aren't obliged to marry me.'

'So I'm not obliged to marry you. Thank you.' Reid's voice chilled her to the bone, and she began to tremble.

'I thought you'd be relieved,' she said wildly, trying to loose his grip. 'After all, as you so rightly said, it isn't as if emotions are involved. . . .'

To her horror he shook her violently until her teeth rattled.

'So everything in the garden's lovely! No embarrassing little consequence to mess up your ordered little life, and goodbye, Reid.'

'No, I didn't mean that.' Kit looked in apprehension at this new Reid. 'Please——'

'Precisely what *did* you mean?' He stared down at her, eyes pale and bright with hostility. 'Now there's no shameful secret to hide I suppose I'm superfluous; is that it? Wedding cancelled.' He twisted a hand painfully in her hair, heedless of the tears that started up in her eyes, and gave a chilling little chuckle. 'Then there's really only one thing to do.'

Kit was crying in earnest by this time.

'What do you mean?' she sobbed, not caring that her eyes were rapidly becoming swollen and the tip of her nose was red. Reid ignored her.

'To be blunt, my fickle darling, if prospective pregnancy is the sole condition necessary to push you into marriage, I'm only too happy to oblige.'

Outraged. Kit somehow managed to get a hand free and slapped him hard across one lean cheek, leaving a red imprint on his skin. There was only an instant to view her handiwork before she was shoved flat on the sofa with Reid's hands tearing at her clothes. She fought, quite literally, tooth and nail, biting at his vengeful mouth, digging her nails into the hard, punitive hands that ignored the frantic opposition she strove to make. Kit's tears dried quickly in the effort to breathe in great gulps of air whenever her mouth was free enough to do so. Eventually she gave up in despair.

'Please, Reid,' she whispered brokenly, 'please don't—hate me.'

The battle was abruptly over. She gave an undignified hiccup as the hands ruthlessly restraining her became caressing and gentle. His tongue licked away a tear and he turned on his side, holding her close against him, soothing and stroking her until she was reasonably calm. When she finally summoned the courage to open her eyes she caught her breath at the expression in Reid's, so close to her own.

'You're an idiot,' he said flatly, 'a goose, a nitwit.'

'Really?' Kit eyed him uncertainly. 'Why?'

'Why, my beautiful ninny, did you think I jumped in eagerly with my plans for matrimony *before* either of us were certain they were necessary?'

'I don't know. . . .' Kit's eyes dropped in confusion. Reid shook his head in sorrow.

'So cool, so intelligent, so self-sufficient—and so dumb!'

'That's an Americanism,' she said disapprovingly.

He shook with laughter, holding her closer.

'No doubt you'll have a brisk little argument with St Peter at the golden gates on the correct choice of words!'

Kit pulled herself together with an effort and sat up, looking about her with displeasure. One shoe was near the door—how did it get over there?—her stockings were in ribbons, a button had departed from her blouse and, without looking, she knew only too well her hair was like a bird's nest.

'Break it to me gently,' she said with a sigh. 'Do I have a black eye again?'

Reid shook his head, lying back with arms behind his head, grinning impenitently.

'Not this time. Besides, to be completely accurate, the black eye wasn't my fault last time round.'

Kit looked doubtful.

'I don't know that I agree. Are you in a hurry to leave?'

Reid was looking at his watch.

'Quite the reverse. When will your family be home?'

'Elevenish.'

'Over an hour yet. Come here.'

The smile that accompanied this invitation played havoc with Kit's fragile composure, and she tried to scramble to her feet, but Reid merely scooped her off her feet and held her full length against him again.

'Now,' he said comfortably, 'what were we talking about?'

'You were cross with me,' said Kit, her voice muffled against his throat.

'Cross! I was bloody furious!' Reid put a finger under her chin and raised her face to his. 'You also said something inaccurate about no emotions being involved, as I recall.'

Kit frowned indignantly.

'You must admit you were horribly businesslike when you suggested marriage; going on about how suitable I was in every way, and that by and large the idea seemed a fairly viable proposition, particularly as at the time there was the possibility of a child as the direct result of your attentions.'

'Katharine,' he said softly, 'for God's sake stop babbling. Just shut up and kiss me.'

She complied with such breathtaking ardour that Reid's much-tried self-control practically deserted him once more.

'Darling,' he muttered eventually, his breathing ragged. 'Do you speak Portuguese?'

'No.' At this moment in time Kit had no interest whatsoever in beginning to learn, either.

'The verb "to love" is "*amar*", but in common speech the verb "*querer*" is used for both love and want, according to context.'

Kit was still looking up into the dark, intense face above hers.

'And?' she prompted softly.

'I've spoken both languages all my life, and until now I've never felt the need to differentiate between the meanings.' He kissed her lightly and smoothed her tangled hair. 'At the risk of boring you I think we're back to semantics again, because I want to make my meaning clear. I want you—which fact is patently obvious at this very moment—but I realise very clearly that I also love you intensely, which is why I'm exercising some not inconsiderable restraint.'

'And all that stuff about suitability and so on?'

'The truth. You are everything any man could ever want.' Reid paused and looked down at her in wonder. 'I can only marvel at the fact that some man hasn't snapped you up before this.'

'Several have tried,' she assured him, smiling at him with a beautiful, new self-confidence. 'But there was never that necessary spark.'

'And now?' He kissed her at length before allowing her to reply.

Kit pushed him away unwillingly and stood up.

'Spark is inadequate, darling. Conflagration comes nearer the mark, and this being the case I'll go and make some repairs before the family come home.' She gave him a luminous smile, and held out her hand. Reid stood up, taking it in his.

'I love you, Reid,' she said, looking at him squarely, 'but I feel I must mention one little thing that disturbs me. To other people you always appear so sort of— together and in command, yet with me you seem subject to these recurrent episodes of near-violence.'

Reid grinned and took her in his arms, rubbing his cheek against hers.

'You are the sole person to cause this particular reaction—my family would never believe you. Not to worry; as long as you are constantly loving, and agree with everything I say, all should be well.'

'In a pig's eye,' countered his beloved, wriggling closer.

'As long as you say "I will" at the appropriate time in church I foresee no problem whatsoever,' he assured her. 'After that everything should be plain sailing.'

'Oh, I will,' said Kit fervently.

'And no fighting afterwards?'

'Well. . . .'

Reid's arms tightened.

'I mean fairly soon afterwards, like our wedding night.'

Kit turned her parted mouth up to his, running the tip of her tongue delicately over his lips.

'What do you think?' she whispered.

His breath rasped as he drew it in unevenly.

'My thoughts at this moment are highly unsuitable to put into words.'

Kit's bubbling laugh was shameless.

'There must be some words, surely!'

Reid bent and whispered in her ear, causing a flood of hot, bright colour to rise in his future wife's face. Miss Katharine Vaughan's entire vocabulary deserted her.

'Oh, Reid,' was all she was able to say, and very faintly at that, after which for some considerable time any words at all were not only unnecessary, but virtually impossible.

Coming Next Month in Harlequin Presents!

703 THE WALL Amanda Carpenter
A lonely Lake Michigan shore seems an unlikely place for a tormented reclusive writer to meet a beautiful singing star. But meet—and love—they do, in this passionate and sensitive romance.

704 DARK PARADISE Sara Craven
For special reasons of her own, a young woman feigns interest in a crusading journalist and accompanies him to the West Indies—where events change her pretend love to the real thing!

705 DANCE WHILE YOU CAN Claire Harrison
A dedicated dancer doesn't have room in her life for love *and* career. So thinks a lovely Manhattan prima ballerina—until a holiday affair with a handsome businessman wreaks havoc with her philosophy.

706 SHADOW MARRIAGE Penny Jordan
Deep in their hearts, an estranged husband and wife, both a part of Hollywood's glamorous film industry, know they need to reconcile to find happiness...yet cruel Fate seems to have other plans.

707 ILLUSION OF LOVE Patricia Lake
An intriguing tale of romance, jealousy and passion that sweeps from a beautiful South Pacific island to an English manor by the sea, and culminates on a luxurious yacht on the French Riviera.

708 GOING UNDERGROUND Karen van der Zee
When a taxing career pushes her to the edge, a young woman spends two months in Virginia helping a handsome single parent with his son. In so doing she discovers her inner strength...and capacity for love.

709 IMPRUDENT CHALLENGE Jessica Steele
A plucky English miss visits her suddenly bankrupt father in Japan to delve into the cause of his financial crisis—only to find herself falling for the very man responsible for it!

710 THE INHERITANCE Kay Thorpe
When an English girl inherits a ranch in Florida, she travels there with the intention of selling...but when she meets, and dislikes on sight, the arrogant would-be buyer, she quickly changes her mind.

Discover the new and unique

Harlequin Gothic and Regency Romance Specials!

Gothic Romance

THE CASTLE
AT JADE COVE
Helen Hicks

AN INNOCENT
MADNESS
Dulcie Hollyock

RESTLESS
OBSESSION
Jane Toombs

Regency Romance

A GENTLEMAN'S
AGREEMENT
Deborah Lynne

REVENGE
FOR A DUCHESS
Sara Orwig

MIDNIGHT FOLLY
Phyllis Pianka

A new and exciting world of romance reading

Harlequin Gothic and Regency Romance Specials!

Available wherever paperback books are sold, or send your name, address and zip or postal code, along with a check or money order for $3.00 for each book ordered (includes 75¢ postage and handling), payable to Harlequin Reader Service, to:

Harlequin Reader Service
In the U.S.
P.O. Box 52040
Phoenix, AZ 85072-9988

In Canada
P.O. Box 2800, Postal Station A
5170 Yonge Street
Willowdale, Ontario M2Z 5T5

CR-2R

Harlequin Celebrates

Thirty-Five Years of Excellence

...and our commitment to excellence continues. Indulge in the pleasure of superb romance reading by choosing the most popular love stories in the world.

Harlequin Presents

Exciting romance novels for the woman of today— a rare blend of passion and dramatic realism.

Harlequin Romance™

Tender, captivating stories that sweep to faraway places and delight with the magic of love.

HARLEQUIN SUPERROMANCE™

Longer, more absorbing love stories for the connoisseur of romantic fiction.

Harlequin Temptation™

Sensual and romantic stories about choices, dilemmas, resolutions, and above all, the fulfillment of love.

Harlequin American Romance™

Contemporary romances— uniquely North American in flavor and appeal.

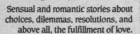

Code: 35-H

Harlequin Photo ~ Calendar ~

Turn Your Favorite Photo into a Calendar.

Uniquely yours, this 10x17½" calendar features your favorite photograph, with any name you wish in attractive lettering at the bottom. A delightfully personal and practical idea!

Send us your favorite color print, black-and-white print, negative, or slide, any size (we'll return it), along with **3** proofs of purchase (coupon below) from a June or July release of Harlequin Romance, Harlequin Presents, Harlequin Superromance Harlequin American Romance or Harlequin Temptation, plus $5.75 (includes shipping and handling).

JULY 1984

The Browns

Harlequin Photo Calendar Offer
(PROOF OF PURCHASE)

NAME_____
(Please Print)

ADDRESS_____

CITY_____ STATE_____ ZIP_____

NAME ON CALENDAR_____

Mail photo, 3 proofs,   **Harlequin Books**   2-
plus check or money order   P.O. Box 52020
for $5.75 payable to: Phoenix, AZ 85072

Offer expires December 31, 1984. (Not available in Canada)   CAL